Lions

Also by Bonnie Nadzam

Lamb

Love in the Anthropocene (with Dale Jamieson)

Lions

a novel

Bonnie Nadzam

Black Cat
New York

Published simultaneously in Canada
Printed in the United States of America

First published by Grove Atlantic, July 2016

FIRST EDITION

ISBN 978-0-8021-2490-6
eISBN 978-0-8021-8991-2

Black Cat
an imprint of Grove Atlantic
154 West 14th Street
New York, NY 10011

Distributed by Publishers Group West

groveatlantic.com

16 17 18 19   10 9 8 7 6 5 4 3 2 1

For my father, Jeffrey Thomas Nadzam,
and for all the good men who do good work

If you've ever really loved anyone, you know there's a ghost in everything. Once you see it, you see it everywhere. It looks out at you from the stillness of a rail-backed chair. From the old 1952 Massey-Harris Pony tractor out front, its once shining red metal now a rust-splotched pink, headlights broken off. No eyes.

Picture high plains in late spring. Green rows of winter wheat combed across the flat, wide-open ground. The derelict sugar beet factory, its thousands of red bricks fenced in by chain-link clotted with Russian thistle. Farther down the two-lane highway, the moon rising like an egg over the hollow grain elevator, rusted at its seams. To the north and west, the sparsely populated town. Golden rectangles of a few lit windows floating above the plain.

They called it Lions, a name meant to stand in for disappointment with the wild invention and unreasonable hope by which it had been first imagined, then sought and spuriously claimed. There were never any lions. In fact there is nothing more to the place now than a hard rind of shimmering dirt and grass. The wind scours it constantly, scrubbing the sage and sweeping out all the deserted buildings and weathered homes, clearing out those that aren't already bare. Flat as hell's basement and empty as the boundless sky above it. The horizon makes as clean and slight a curve as if lathed by a master craftsman. Nothing is hidden.

And yet.

It's said that in naming the place after a dream from which they refused to awaken, the people of Lions put a curse upon themselves as much as on the town itself—one that finally ripened the summer a man and his dog came walking into town along the bar ditch from God knew where, his dark clothes blowing like robes in the wind.

He must have been from up north, people said.

Circled around on foot over the buttes, then hit the highway and came in as if he were from the east.

Didn't want anyone to know where he was from, they said. Or what he was doing.

They say that later that night, when Chuck Garcia, the county sheriff, asked him who he was, this man could give no answer. No name, no ID, and a shrug of his shoulders. They say he was gaunt, his face oddly shadowed, and that even though by the gray in his hair and the stoop of his shoulders they guessed him to be fifty, fifty-five years old, he had not a line in his face, nor any light in his eyes, which were black as seeds.

They say that just after this man stopped at the Walkers', John Walker practically keeled over dead where he stood, and Georgianna, his beloved wife of thirty-five years, all but evaporated from the kitchen at the back of the house, so distant and unearthly did she seem to become. They say that Gordon, their son, left alone to pick up the pieces and carry on his father's work, was doomed.

Leigh Ransom, who was seventeen when what seemed like the perfect summer began, had known something like this was coming. Close as she was to the Walkers, she of course knew the details of John Walker's own father suddenly dying, years ago, and could have predicted something similar would happen to John himself. There were patterns to things, especially in places like Lions. Especially when you were talking about the Walkers. So when she saw the silent ambulance lights from her bedroom that night, she knew whom they'd come for. She knew what was beginning to unfold. She could picture it all: the faded periwinkles on Georgianna's cotton nightgown as John woke beside her in a nauseated sweat; the runny moonlight in their bedroom, shadows of the framed window printed slantwise across the old hardwood floor; John Walker's hand, cold and damp, suddenly clenching the top of Georgianna's thigh beneath the sheets; his swaying—he missed a step, then another—and their dance together down the narrow staircase to the front door, where he fell on the tile in his T-shirt and underwear, his blue jeans draped over her arm.

And if anybody had asked her that night, Leigh could have described everything that would happen to Gordon in the days ahead, as a result. How in the Burnsville clinic the next morning, the nurse would fold her hands at her wide belly, the toes of her white tennis shoes pointed outward, her hair cut in a smooth iron gray helmet, her blue eyes dull and bloodshot. Outside the windows, a violet green swallow piping in one of the landscaped trees. Inside, computers and medical devices clicking, hushed voices drifting and gathering around the triage station. Rubber-bottomed safety shoes squeaking on the polished floor.

Gordon would stand in the clinic hallway holding a white paper takeout bag from the diner in Lions as the floor tilted and the door to his father's room contracted into a small rectangle as if suddenly drawn some immeasurable distance away.

"You'll want to say your good-byes," the nurse would tell him and Georgianna in an even voice. "I am so sorry. He's not likely to regain consciousness."

But when Gordon was alone with him later that hour, that's exactly what his father would do, making a low hum in the back of his throat, clearing it to speak, as he opened his eyes. He'd speak slowly, interrupted with long periods of silence, between cycles of the ventilator. Clear fluid in the IV bag shimmering in the gray light. The electrocardiography machine beeping at regular intervals.

"Write this down," John Walker would say, reciting the instructions by heart as Gordon took notes on the back of a Gas & Grocer receipt in his wallet, then describing the task he was asking his son to perform. Afterward he would pause, looking out the window from his bed at the silver poplar. "You can say no, Gordon. But this has been my life's work. And one way or another, it will be yours."

Here was a master of his craft who built a first-class weld servicing facility, who spent ten hours of every workday in his shop, whom Leigh had heard people say could outweld even the Hobart and Lincoln Electric sales engineers working the region, who was famous in eastern Colorado for his skill and precision, but who was calling his life's work this odd errand out of town to deliver canned food, blankets, candles, batteries, and firewood to somebody up north.

"Don't speed," he'd tell Gordon. "Don't look for shortcuts. If you find you've made a wrong turn, go back to the place where you went astray and start again from there. Remember when you're up there that I ran the same errand myself for thirty-five years, and was never the worse for it. Whatever you might hear to the contrary."

And Gordon would know what his father meant—what people sometimes said of John Walker, of the Walker men before him, and what they would come to say of Gordon. He'd know what his father's request would do to his life, the one he thought he'd have, the one he was on the edge of taking up in his hands that summer, the one with her. They were going to leave. But as Gordon stood there in the hospital room looking down at his father, neither the rumors, his plans, nor the cost of ignoring them would matter.

And so from that first night and all through the summer as Leigh walked from her mother's diner to her bedroom to the empty factory to the Walkers' house and back again, the sun broiling her neck and the top of her head, waiting for Gordon to reappear after an absence of a week or three nights or five, she tried to understand how these Walkers, who lived so small, and had seemed so good, ended up at the heart of a story like this one.

Story goes, when the man and his dog came down off the edge of the highway into town, they crossed the unpaved frontage road and stepped over the fallen fence posts toward a little white house—the Walkers'.

He stopped next to the frame of a rusted old tomato-red Bronco someone had dropped off for Gordon or John to clean up and repair, but had never returned to claim. A hundred feet from the house was the Walkers' shop, its windows open to the narrow county road where the Gas & Grocer had stood sixty-one years, and next door to that, May and Leigh Ransom's little place.

It was just barely twilight. The man stooped and scratched the dog behind the ears and spoke to her, looking out over what he could see of town. From the slight inclination of the plain, it must have appeared a shipwreck awash in grass—the old splintered homesteads half sunk in dirt, the small crush of lights in the distance from the diner and the bar where anyone still surviving had gathered together to ride out the coming night.

He circled around the Walkers' weld shop—a combination pole barn and Quonset hut surrounded by neat piles of scrap metal and corrugated steel. It was filled with pretty fine machinery and tools for repairing broken farm equipment and assembling hog fencing. In various forms, the shop belonged to John Walker, his father, William, grandfather Charles, and another two Johns, before them, the first opening his doors primarily as a wheelwright in the nineteenth century right around the time Lions was founded. So did Gordon's paternal grandfathers reach back in the history of the county as agricultural equipment innovators and repairmen. They had never been cowboys, they had never been hunters or trappers, they had never been traders or soldiers, and they had never been farmers—not even in the days when it seemed every man west of the 90th meridian was some combination of them all. They had long been the only metalworkers in the region, as far back as living memory went, and always with expertise far beyond the meager needs of the county.

John Walker in particular was a masterful and efficient welder, with skill in proportion to his oddness. If there was a wildfire in the foothills or in the mountains, he knew it first. If it was going to rain in a day's time, he had already tacked down the tarps over the hay at Dock Sterling's place, before Dock himself could see to it. His neighbors mistook for queer perspicacity what was in fact great attention, and what his wife called serious love.

The Walkers were strange like that, they said. Hard to figure.

But good guys. Reliable.

Heck. John'd do anything for you.

They'd all raise their glasses to that.

But no common sense, they agreed, and the men shook their heads. The women—heavy around the middle, slender gold crosses around their necks, and hair colored from boxes of dye they bought at the grocery store in Burnsville—all looked away, out the window to the empty street and storefronts that made up the single block of downtown. The mute television hanging over the bar flashed a commercial for car insurance.

As if the man had no interest in money, someone said.

They were all like that, someone said. All the Walkers.

For example, decades before it was common practice, Gordon's great-grandfather fashioned a manner of swather out of scrap. It cut the grain and laid it on the ground in windrows, allowing it to dry before harvest. It was by this invention that Lions finally for a brief uncharacteristically rainy decade seemed to promise a little prosperity. This great-grandfather Charles never thought of patenting the swather, however, so never profited by it in any worldly sense. He'd bent over the metal with some design in mind, to help a neighbor who was a distant cousin on his wife's side, and considered a more efficient harvest payment enough. Sons and daughters of those neighboring farmers whom he helped accumulate a little wealth soon moved on to Denver, Salt Lake, Phoenix, and San Diego, where their great-grandsons and -granddaughters now live in flat-faced stucco houses on smooth, curved streets that you will discover, if you are a careful student of cartography, loop into the interstates and highways in broad, swooping, endless circles.

If what this New World offered was boundless opportunity for material wealth—reward for ambition and grit—then it really was a mystery why any of the Walkers came to the continent in the first place. Of course there may have been some exchange of perishable goods for the rudimentary swather: a season's worth of fresh eggs, or clay jars of alfalfa honey, or plums or cherries, which every few summers grew with an abundance the early farmers could neither predict nor control, and which were otherwise impossible to come by. Some things—carrots, potatoes, turnips—you could keep in ten-gallon buckets of cold sand in a dirt cellar straight through the winter, but fresh fruit was rare. Gordon's grandmother, if left alone for an afternoon, might be discovered beneath the warty hackberry tree, her kitchen work and laundry left undone, indolently eating a lapful of plums, one after another, sticky pink juice running down her chin and neck and wrists and forearms, flyaway dark hair standing out in a frayed and sweaty halo around her face.

Look, she would say, I love these plums. And love is never idle.

The Walkers' was the first house the man on the highway would have seen when he dipped down onto the frontage road at the exit to town. Perhaps it was only because of this that he felt welcomed by the small, tidy home and crossed the weeds and clipped grass to the back door.

Perhaps it was that simple.

Georgianna Walker was ready for him with a mug of hot black coffee. Her long, gray hair was parted in the middle and pinned up behind her ears in tin barrettes, her face scrubbed clean.

"All out of change," the man said, putting his hands up.

"Please." She extended the cup to the stranger, and when he took it, she ushered him inside and pulled out a kitchen chair. "You're just in time for dinner. Scrambled eggs, buttered toast, and cocoa sound good?"

He checked her face and she nodded and smiled. He sat down. "Almost a warm spring night," he said.

"We're getting there. Couple weeks it'll be hotter than we can stand."

"That's a good-looking dog," John Walker said coming out of the living room, grinning, his finger holding the place in a paperback. "What's its name?"

The man looked across the room at him. "That's my Sadie."

"Come a long way together?"

"All the way together."

"Will she eat eggs?"

"We'd both eat eggs."

John set the paperback open, facedown, on a shelf beside the pantry door.

"Good story?" the man asked.

John smiled. "Old cowboy book my dad used to read." He picked it back up and turned the cover to show the visitor. It featured a man on horseback in a long yellow linen duster. The horse was black with a fiery red eye, and rearing on its back legs. In the distance, a snake behind a sage bush, and a woman in a turquoise dress pouring off her shoulders like water.

Both men laughed.

"I don't know that one," the man said.

John had a hundred more with covers just like it: a bearded man crouched in a mountain stream and panning for gold, an outlaw with a red bandanna tied over his face and a pistol in hand, creeping up from behind; a shoot-out in a dusty street; a magnificent cowboy on horseback draped in curtains of blue snow, long ribbons of the dark and wild mane of his dark and wild horse whipping sideways in a glacial wind.

Georgianna took out the eggs, milk, and bread, while John led the man upstairs to the shower and found him an old pair of coveralls carefully patched with scrap denim. Dressed in the borrowed clothes while the washing machine churned his dirty ones—Georgianna had given him no choice in the matter—the man sat back in his kitchen chair. Neither John nor Georgianna asked anything of him, not his name and not a story, nor did the man offer anything.

All of this Chuck relayed weeks later at the bar, and the report made the men and women shake their heads.

The Walkers, God.

"You didn't ask him anything? Who he was? Where he was from?" Chuck inquired of John the evening after the stranger disappeared. He wrapped his fingers around the warm coffee mug and leaned forward in the kitchen chair. Georgianna set a thick slice of yellow pound cake before him.

John shrugged. "He needed a shower and a meal."

Chuck smiled at his old neighbor and cut into the cake with his fork. "Well. At least you didn't keep him."

"He said he couldn't stay."

Couldn't stay.

Can you imagine?

Bringing a man off the highway like that into your home?

With your wife and son?

He could've been sick.

He could've been on the run.

It's a nice enough impulse but my God. You got to be more careful than that these days.

Could've been a thief, a drunk, or worse.

Could've been a foreigner.

He *looked* like a foreigner.

Anything could have happened.

They tsked, they looked at each other with faces of wonder. They never could understand John Walker or what seemed to be his lifetime of poor decision making. The backward code he seemed to live and work by—his entrepreneurial failure somehow as perpetual as it was absolute. It was as if each of the Walkers in his time was choosing again and again, every morning in his workshirt with his first cup of coffee, to fail. They worked for free, or seemed to; they forgot or neglected to bill their neighbors; they worked so many hours a day, but scarcely profited by it at all.

What other, secret work did these Walkers live on?

People wondered. People talked.

John Walker. Just look at the guy.

That long, lean frame, the patched workshirt, the steel-toed boots. And that look in his eye, as if he had seen right behind your face and into the inner workings of your brain and had decided, upon seeing everything there was to see about you, to say nothing. A nod of the head.

And Gordon. Did you ever see a more serious eighteen-year-old?

Works harder than three grown men put together.

Abnormal, tell you what.

Yeah but he's got Leigh Ransom's attention.

A knowing look, a groan.

In such a small town she seemed a great beauty, her hair long and brownish gold and tumbling over her shoulders and down her back the way the g and the h fell with bulky grace through the letters of her name.

Gordon must be hung like a bull, someone said.

Everyone laughed.

That girl is vain about her hair.

All women are vain about their hair.

And then there was John Walker's regular disappearance out of town, presumably to tend remote customers up near Three

Bells or Horses, customers who, if they really existed, were probably not paying him for his work, either.

Walkers used to run a farrier service out of their old trucks, someone remembered.

Yeah, but no one up north has horses anymore.

No one up there has anything anymore.

Nothing up there but an old gas station. Used to belong to that Indian guy with no teeth.

Gerald. But he wasn't an Indian. He'd make you an RC with whiskey.

Sharp as a tack.

Whatever happened to him?

A shrug.

Well anyway, gone now. Nothing and no one up there.

See then? Walker's visiting Boggs. Got to be.

More laughter.

So had they sometimes jokingly cast John Walker as the unlucky Good Samaritan of local legend in which a man and all of his sons and grandsons were bound through the generations to tend an immortal, wounded pioneer, one Lamar Boggs, purportedly left for dead by his nineteenth-century companions who were racing west like hell for leather after a better life. The first Walker in the region found him, nursed him, and set him up safe and sound in a tiny hut on the mesa. One you could still find if you drove north, and were really looking for it.

And truth be told, the joke sort of stood to reason. In over a hundred years—in spite of all rationale and opportunity as their neighbors fled drought, dust, influenza, auctioneers, grasshoppers, fire, boredom, and disappointment—the Walkers never left Lions. If there were other stragglers in town, it was because they didn't have the means to leave, or weren't staying permanently, but working various financial stratagems to land someplace better. Denver, say, or Boise. They liked to say to each other in Lions that those who had come to America and come west, as their families had, did so because they were risk takers and big dreamers. But what, they wondered, had been the Walkers' dream? For what had they taken the risk of coming out here and then, against all reason, decided to stay? They might have thrived somewhere else, but were riveted to the plain, it seemed, couldn't leave if they'd wanted to. If old Boggs was really up there, the Walkers were certainly the men to tend him.

"No one else would stick around to do it," Boyd Hardy said. He stood behind the bar with arms folded in front of his chest, a bottle of Bud Light in one hand, leaning back against the counter.

"Tell you what," Dock said, and pointed his beer bottle in Boyd's direction. "If they weren't the best men in the county I'd say you had it wrong."

"Maybe he just goes north to be alone," May Ransom said from behind the bar, where she often ended up after closing her diner across the street. She refilled her own glass of boxed white wine.

Boyd stared outside, not moving. "Seems to me there's alone enough to be had right here in town."

When weeks later Chuck told them about the stranger's stop at the Walkers' that night—the shower, the cocoa, the buttered toast—everyone shot accusatory looks at Boyd, who by that time was a little hangdog, his thick silver mustache a little ragged, his own truck oiled up and ready to pack and leave Lions for good.

"You all saw him," Boyd said.

Yes, they'd all seen him.

But that evening in the Walkers' kitchen, the man had bent over the table with John and Georgianna and spooned scrambled eggs into his mouth, perfectly sound, perfectly human, if the Walkers and Chuck could be believed.

They'd talked about the country, Chuck reported, and the stranger spoke like a stranger indeed, full of questions about what they grew in town, and for how long, and how it was that this little place tacked to the high plains had managed to survive.

"Does it look like it survived?" Georgianna asked, and smiled.

According to Chuck, they talked snowmelt, irrigation, alfalfa, hog feed, and welding. The man had a cousin who was a metalworker, and who would have envied John's setup to no end.

"A metalworker," John said, grinning and displaying his evenly gapped teeth.

The man wiped his index finger across the plate to get all the yolk and licked it clean. "Beg your pardon, ma'am." He set his hands in his lap. "Been hungry."

Georgianna was back up at the stove. She set two warm hard-boiled eggs on the counter beside her. "For your Sadie," she said.

"Thank you."

"And another couple for you coming up, no arguments."

"Thank you so much." He spread his long hands open on the kitchen table and stood.

To the west the sky was slowly darkening to blue-black and the box elder branches were beginning to circle and twist in the increasing wind.

"Warming up to rain," John said, "but it won't rain." It had rained a week earlier, a thin and drizzly sputter that would turn out to be the last until mid-October when a cold and wet turn of weather would freeze into sheets of jagged glass across the plain.

John and Georgianna stood beside each other inside the window, watching the man carry both eggs in one hand across the grass to his dog. She wagged her tail as the man approached and took each egg, one at a time, into her mouth. Then the man stooped and spoke to her, scratched her ears. John put his hand on the small of his wife's back.

When the man returned to the house he thanked them again. "Feels good to give your traveling companion something good to eat." Then he ate four more eggs—eight eggs in that single meal.

"Been out in the snow and weather much?" John asked him.

"Some."

"You have the things you need? Want a thermos? Got an extra in the shop."

"A warm hat," Georgianna said.

The man raised an open hand in their direction and shook his head. "Something I can do for you?"

Outside in the wind and last light he helped John move a pile of corrugated steel scavenged from a demolished farmhouse and its outbuildings twenty miles north, in Horses. They both wore heavy gloves and sidestepped through the new weeds until the pile was in the pole barn. They put the scrap angle iron and rectangular tubing on racks. The dog circled the men and pounced on field mice and loosed a skein of red-winged black-birds that lifted up over the house and settled again behind it. Back in the kitchen the men washed their hands in the sink and a cold blast of wind blew the curtains in. Georgianna reached across the stranger and closed the window with a long, freckled arm. "Looks like you found us just in time," she said. "Why don't you bring your dog in?"

"In the house?"

"We'll set you up on the cot in the bunkroom for the night," John said. "It's nothing fancy but it's got a stove. We have another room in the house but it's Gordon's."

"Our son," Georgianna explained. "He's out with his girl."

The man glanced at her, then John. Their open faces, their warm, comfortable home.

"I think best," he said, "if we keep moving."

Georgianna gave him two peanut butter sandwiches, a bag of dried apple rings, and a can of tuna fish for the dog, and put it all with his clean clothes in a plastic bag.

He looked down at the coveralls.

"You keep them," Georgianna said. "Might have a string of cool nights here. Those are sturdy."

John gave the man a ten-dollar bill. By full dark he was walking down the frontage road straight toward town.

At the bar and in the diner, however, given what they learned later, they could hardly believe the man's visit at the Walkers' had been as civil as Chuck's reports indicated it was.

Over the following few weeks, reports of what happened next rushed in whispers like wind through the grass. Edie Jacks, who lived in the house behind the alley, said the man left his dog on a little brown square of withered grass right by Boyd's bar, and opened the door. From her kitchen window where she stood watching, the light inside the bar narrowed to a ribbon and went out.

That evening, Gordon Walker and Leigh Ransom were out in John's truck. Gordon turned north, then west on a narrow county road, and drove straight over a vacant field. The old, blue Silverado bounced and he and Leigh swayed in the cab, but the MIG welder and toolbox were fixed firmly in the bed. In the distance before them, the dark red form of the empty sugar beet factory was set on the ragged edge of town, backed up against what had once been the westernmost edge of fertile tallgrass prairie, then beet fields, and was at last cast aside as hard ribbed ground grown wild with weeds and bristling forbs not even sheep would graze on.

Gordon and Leigh could hike to the factory on foot from their adjacent backyards, but they'd driven out to Burnsville this evening—the closest city, where their high school was—to buy butter burgers and french fries. In the back of the truck, in a cooler, they had a stash of canned beer from Boyd's bar. Leigh ate the last of the fries with her bare feet braced against the passenger door, her head in Gordon's lap so she could see the birds and bats darting above. She reached up with every other fry and popped it into Gordon's mouth as he drove. With each one, she listed something they would have in the fall, in college, that they did not and could not have in Lions.

"People our age," she said.

He glanced down at her. "I only have eyes for you."

"Movie theater."

"Overrated."

"Real restaurants."

"Overpriced."

"Beautiful houses. Museums. Schools. Kayaking. Hiking. Snow on the mountains."

Gordon tossed his hand, dismissing all of it. "Admit it. You love it here. Nowhere else will ever compare."

She pinched him. "Stop. I know you want to go."

He ran his fingertips along her jaw and rested his hand on her shoulder. "I do," he said. "Of course I do." He slowed the truck to a stop, turned off the engine, pulled her up, and kissed the sides of her face.

To get inside the factory they went not over the razor wire, but beneath a curled lip of chain-link that as children they'd disguised by tacking it back down with a railroad spike in a hole that took all day to pick out, the pale dirt so hard and dry it was no more fertile than moon rock. They say in its first years of being tilled there were nearly a hundred kinds of wheat growing in the county, and fifty kinds of oats, and flowering fields of green and white alfalfa of such prodigious harvests that at the World's Fair grand prizes for both comb and strained alfalfa honey went to Lions. They say the nights were uniformly cool and the days were full of sunshine, that there was no such thing as mud or dust, only loamy black soil the consistency of dense chocolate cake, and root vegetables as big as your head. Some of the old-timers, however, might snort and tell you such stories don't amount to much more than how a sense of loss can lead a person to imagine an overabundant past. If for a short time the story people told themselves about the place involved bushels of grain, melons big as wagon wheels, and ten-pound sugar beets, so much the worse for the ground that yielded them. Where once there had been wild onions and yams, buffalo, antelope, bears, and streams of fish, Lions' earliest residents envisioned cattle, wheat, hog feed, expansive homes. When the former were decimated, the place became inhospitable, the sun hostile, the dirt shallow and as fine and dry as chaff. Their mistake was not in failing to see how difficult it would be to turn the place into a garden, but in failing to see that it had already been one when they arrived.

Sometimes when Leigh stepped inside the dim and rosy light of the empty factory, she felt something touch the back of her shoulder as if to warn her away. She was conscious of whispers and shadows moving across the wall, pricked by a nagging feeling not so much of alarm, or of fear, but of naked longing. The kind of feeling you get when you see the taillights of a single car disappearing over the curved ridge of earth in the last light of day. Wasn't it pulling something of yourself along with it? There was a powerful spirit in the factory, she tried to tell Gordon. Something unsettled, a darkness that felt alive despite its stillness. He asked her to point to it. She slapped at him.

What had been the second-story floor had begun to buckle and crack, so that sun and moonlight splintered at odd angles in strange, bright patterns overhead. It was old flatiron construction, with massive beams of riveted steel. Broken slatted boards were nailed and rotting over long, narrow arched windows. On more than one occasion the feeling the place gave Leigh raised the hair on her forearms and scared her outside. Once Gordon not only laughed at her, he planted his feet, threw his head back, and asked whatever was there if it wouldn't show its face. Come out of hiding.

"It will kill you," she whispered from the doorway.

"If it's so important," he said, "ignoring it will kill you."

Only one man's story from the factory survived from the days before it finally shut down, if you could trust Marybeth Sharpe, now ninety-three years old and still living above her junk shop next to the bar. The man was from Rushville, Nebraska, or maybe it was Valentine or Alliance, Marybeth couldn't quite recall, but some small town up there where she had cousins on her father's side. The factory and fields employed scores of men and women to crawl on hands and knees from April to November thinning and blocking the rows to make space for big beets, to maximize teaspoons of sugar per vegetable—it was crippling work—but the Rushville man was lucky. He was neither a Mexican nor a German-Russian immigrant, so his job was inside.

The factory was the same maze of pipes, diffusion cells, flumes, and tanks you'd find in there today, but all the steel now rust-bitten and corroded was at that time a bright blue metal. Rushville's job was on the first floor of the north side, where great agitators blended sugar beet juice with lime. He was to produce the lime rock in a massive coke oven. Around him in stacks of red brick and twists of metal were narrow metal staircases and fires, hot water, towers of steam. The decaying beet mash in the plumbing stank like hellrot, and where it landed outside of the plumbing it slicked every walking surface with slime. On a day when the graining screens malfunctioned, which was common enough, Rushville was on shift. He shut off the steam and began disassembling the heating drum, but when he unfastened the bolts, gallons of scalding water poured out over him from above.

You can imagine the screams of steam, the screams from the man, the terror in the hearts of his fellow workers, who would have been torn between helping and shielding themselves. Outside in the fields, the men and women stopped crawling over the bony soil and listened. The sun roared down on them.

In most versions of the story, Rushville did not die. Years after the accident, after he had healed from the immediate burns and skin grew over him in a sheen of pink plasticky flesh, his face unrecognizable, his hands missing most of their fingers, his wife birthed a baby girl.

It was the bundle of these last few details that haunted Gordon and Leigh, the white ovals of their faces uplifted in the dusty junk shop as Marybeth described the strange little family and the long, low, dilapidated potato barn they inhabited. Thinking of the transformation of that man, of all the mornings he woke without a face anyone would recognize as human, missing pieces of his hands, his arms immobilized by hardening scar tissue. Imagine him, this man, making love to his wife. What mettle or faith must have been required of her? And not just required of her, but of him, and of their daughter, too, who never left them, and, it was said, was buried beside them?

"Staying power," Marybeth Sharpe said, her twisted-up hair already white as bone. "This was a good man," she said. "You understand? And a very good woman." She pointed her eyes and nose at each of them, one after another. "OK. Get out. That's all you need to know."

Sometimes in the factory with nothing better to do, as tonight, Leigh remembered Rushville in a ceremony of her own design, in order to ward off such tragedy. It was not so much an act of faith as part of a bargain: in exchange for the time the ceremony took from her life was a promise that things would go well for her, that all the rumors of abundance and health and wealth and progress would be bestowed upon her. Good fortune would come to her precisely because she had taken the time to perform this liturgy, one that would keep her safe and happy because she'd written it that way.

In the factory, she kept blindfolds. A fistful of bruised weeds—thistle and toadflax and knapweed—for fragrance. Tonight, the light was changing outside the window from blue to black. The wind was picking up. A nightjar purred in the dead box elder tree, clenched like a bony hand against the evening sky. All these things had their place.

Leigh and Gordon sat crosslegged on the concrete in the dust, knee to knee to knee to knee, and tied torn scraps of threadbare pillowcases around their eyes, knotting them at the backs of their heads. Gordon reached up first, and touched Leigh's cheekbone. She returned a touch in the same place on his own face: right cheekbone. Their hands floated in the darkening room from one body part to another. A single white-throated swift darted above them and swooped out into the blue square of light. She touched his chin. He touched her chin, then opened his hand on the crown of her head. Crown of his head. Bottom of her feet, left then right, until they touched each other everywhere Marybeth had told them the man had been burned. They touched each other purposefully and lightly, with a brush of fingers as soft as fescue when you're stretched out in the summer grass, and the day is as long as a season, the season as long as a year.

When they finished and removed their blindfolds, her eyes were misty. Gordon laughed at her.

"I just like to touch that place on your throat." He stood and pulled her up.

"You have to put your heart into it, Gordon. Or something bad will happen to you."

Gordon knocked on her head. She snatched his fist and bit his knuckles.

"So superstitious," he said.

"You really want to risk being wrong?"

"Now you're getting religious on me."

"I am not." She set a gold can of beer in his hand and opened one of her own. They stood looking out the third-story window. He put his nose in her hair.

"I wish we had some better beer," she said. "Tell you what, when we drive out of here I'm never having another one of these. Ever."

"What will you have? Let me guess. Champagne, three times a day. And big boats of ice cream."

"Yes. We'll go out."

"Sure."

"We'll bring our books and drink coffee."

"What'll we read?"

"Everything."

"That's a lot of homework."

"I'll read half of everything, and you read the other half." He pulled her in closer.

"Do you think other people have it like this?" she asked.

"What other people?"

"The people in Burnsville," she said. "Like Katie and Cody. Do you think they have it like this?"

"There are no people in Burnsville."

"But you've seen them!"

"I don't see them now." He turned her around to face him and she set her beer down on the rotted windowsill and interlaced her fingers behind his back. In their intimacy there was a line they had not yet crossed, and while Gordon always stopped himself short, saying they belonged to each other, and they didn't have to hurry, she always had the sense that he meant something else: that although she was his, he was not entirely hers. He was reserved for something else, just out of her reach.

Inside the bar it was dark and sticky and smelled of yeast and cigarette smoke. To the front were two pane windows on either side of a heavy, insulated wooden door, thick with a hundred layers of finish, grease, and weather, with a great big dirty brass handle. The walls were covered with framed photographs of the past fifty years, long before the bar was Boyd's. Bird hunters in camouflage and neon orange stooped in the brown grass beside their liver-colored bird dogs; football players in shining helmets from the days before Lions' schools were closed; soldiers; rodeo queens; parade floats; 4-H winners with their blue-ribboned hogs and gooseberry preserves. A ratty old wooden sign—Boyd only kept it up because it was funny, he said—painted with the words "No dogs and No Indians." Above the bar, the skin from a three-foot-long rattler that they said someone had killed with his bare hands had been glued to poster board and framed, but it was crumbling behind the glass. The floor was poured concrete and the walls were painted red, white, blue, and gold. Beer colors, Boyd had said.

The man from the highway went up to the bar and ordered one.

It was Boyd himself, turned outward on his stool and stroking his thick silver mustache, who pointed at the coveralls when the stranger sat down at the bar that night. He'd been in the middle of a joke about taxes, immigrants, and an old Mexican woman. Harmless given the company, he kidded, everyone was white in Lions except Chuck Garcia, whom he liked to call Carlos, but whose name was Chuck. Not Charles, not Carlos. And Chuck wasn't even in the house at the time.

He nodded at the coveralls on the odd-looking stranger. "Case in point," Boyd said. "Those are Walker's." Any mustard-colored, pin-hole-burned, and fastidiously patched coveralls in the county were John's or Gordon's.

May had already closed up the diner across the street and was helping out behind the bar, mostly—as usual—to keep an eye on how much Boyd took down himself. So it was she who handed the man the drink he'd asked for before she walked out to the tables to gather empties.

The man ignored Boyd's comment and drank the foam off the beer. Boyd leaned on the bar, right next to him. The man set the glass down and straightened.

Yes, they were Walker's coveralls. John was the kind of man who would help out a passerby. Many of the men and women in the bar that night had depended on him for such, in various ways, over the years. One of them, Haley Netterson, had even lived in the bunkhouse attached to the Quonset hut for nearly a year. John and Gordon had welded together the pedestal-mounted woodstove in there just to keep her through the cold weather, and hauled in a truckload of wood from the mountains they'd bucked up and split themselves. Stacked it right outside the little, steel-backed door, beside the twin bed, so she wouldn't have to walk into the snow or smack of cold morning air to get it. Georgianna put a red painted iron kettle on the stove, and little blue-checked curtains over a single window.

"Probably gave you a handout for your beer, too," Boyd said to the man, glancing around for encouragement. "Am I right?"

May whipped at him with a damp rag. "Shut your mouth."

"Communal glass of beer," someone said.

"Guess where the old Mexican lady put it."

A few laughs.

The stranger sat still, his long face pointed at the spotted mirror and rows of colored glass bottles, his arms hanging at his sides, his fingers twitching at the ends of his hands.

Not exactly a natural way to sit at a bar, they said later.

Nothing natural about that man.

Felt something funny the moment he walked in.

Boyd picked up the man's beer and took a drink, or pretended to take a drink. "Just as easily call it mine," he said.

"Alright Boyd," May said. "Enough."

The man looked down at his lap and Boyd moved to pour the beer over the man's head. Of course Boyd never would have done it. He was in high form. Maybe he'd had one too many, but it was only meant to punctuate his joke, this feint, and everyone pretty much believed that. He could be a bully and an ass, he could be moody and sullen one minute and the life of the town the next, but Boyd Hardy wasn't mean. Besides, it was his bar. No reasonable man wanted trouble in his own bar.

Just giving the poor old son of a bitch a hard time, he'd say later whenever it came up. But at that point, Boyd had not yet finished his joke, and the anticipation of the small audience was too much. They were all three or four glasses in, and there was no place else to go that night but home, and home wasn't a place anybody in Lions wanted to be.

Say Boyd tipped the man's glass this way and that, sloshing it just a little too close to one of the man's shoulders. Perhaps the man stood and in one smooth, easy motion knocked Boyd Hardy off his stool, which sailed through the air and cracked the window beside the front door, a crack like a river that slowly spread imperceptibly in fine tributaries in the days and weeks ahead.

Or perhaps it was that the gesture—the beer held for a moment over the man's head—so alarmed May that she got hold of Boyd's arm first. The pint glass dropped and shattered on the concrete floor. Falling off his stool, Boyd jerked away from May, who fell back on her tailbone and bit her tongue. Dock Sterling said that even from where he was sitting, and even knowing what he knew about Boyd and May, it looked like Boyd had struck her.

Boyd wouldn't have dared. No one would hit May. She had been a real beauty in her day and had learned to use it to her advantage, so that even at fifty she had some considerable leverage over the men in town, though most of them remembered her in her twenties, too, and the memory alone would've been enough to make them behave. However else her life had disappointed her, as she sometimes intimated it had, in Lions she always had a sharp tongue and the upper hand.

The way one woman in the bar told it, May stood up with blood on her chin and watched as the stranger rose. In a moment the stool he'd been sitting on and Boyd too were on the other side of the room, the pane window beside the door cracked. The woman couldn't say who had thrown what.

Levon, from the garage, said the man stood and tried to leave after knocking both Boyd and May to the ground, and that it was Boyd who threw the stool, hitting the stranger behind the knee and accounting for the limp others said they saw as he dragged a leg behind him the following morning.

In any case, the tall man from the highway was on his feet, the bar was in some general confusion, Boyd was swearing and bleeding from a small cut along his hairline, and Chuck pulled up to the bar in his police car, believing his work for the night was over. When Chuck took the man with him, the man called into the bar something about a dog out back, which was taken to be an insult directed at Boyd.

In the morning there was a bruise on Boyd's cheekbone like a smudge of soot that for a full month seemed neither to change nor to fade. This was a sign, some people said.

"He's going to come back and burn the place down," Dock suggested, his big pink cheeks flushed and baby blue eyes deadly serious.

Boyd dismissed this with a wave of his hand.

"You watch," Dock said. "He'll burn us out."

"Like hell," Boyd said, touching his cheek, neither believing nor disbelieving.

After all, it was true. You had to read the signs. It was how you survived, wasn't it?

A stand of tall grass, broken.

A misplaced dish.

An oddness in the room.

That this stranger in Lions had been unnecessarily violent and hence had sealed his own fate seemed defensible. But whenever anyone said so, there was a palpable unease, a quiet moment afterward when everyone at the bar raised their glasses to their lips.

He went willingly to the Lions jail—two rooms off the back of Chuck's local office—and once inside and seated, with what Chuck called dead eyes and a dead face, the man said his name was John Doe. He had no form of identification. He admitted he may have caused some trouble in the bar. Chuck looked down at the paperwork in front of him and set down his pen. The memory of this eerie exchange kept him awake for a string of nights in mid-July when heat lightning fanned out in the distance beyond his yard and the lamplight burned yellow on the cardboard boxes his wife had begun packing with sheets, towels, teacups, books, and all the domestic odds and ends they'd accumulated in their twenty-seven years in the house.

In his office that night Chuck searched the man, found his newly cleaned clothes, the apple rings and peanut butter sandwiches, found the ten-dollar bill, and found a photograph of a narrow house stamped with the address of a photography store, Nel's Camera, in North Platte, Nebraska. Had he walked the whole way from Nebraska?

The man considered a moment and shifted in his chair.

"Didn't anyone give you a ride?" Chuck asked.

"Wasn't looking for one."

"What were you looking for?"

But the man did not, or could not, say.

"Tell me I don't need to make any calls to North Platte," Chuck said, but even before it was out he was sorry he said it. Beside him, the man put trembling fingers to his forehead and looked down at the floor. It was the look and gesture of a man who had lost everything. Chuck had seen it before. Now he turned away. He'd inquire with the guys in North Platte privately, later in the week. None of this had to be official. It'd been a confusing scene in the bar, Boyd had come out bleeding but no real harm done. They'd get it all sorted out in the morning.

He showed the man into the cell with a single cot and toilet. "Warm and dry, anyway. Might rain."

"It won't rain."

The man went in without another word, stepped through the doorway and stopped with his back to Chuck, so that Chuck had to lock the door on him like that.

At midnight, Chuck woke beside his wife in a cold sweat. He started and cried out.

"What is it?" she said, setting her hand on his chest.

He relaxed into his pillow. "Something chasing me."

"Ohh," she said, in the tender way she sometimes soothed him, as if he were a child.

He patted the back of her hand with his fingertips and rose.

"Where are you going?"

"Ssh," he said softly. "Go back to sleep."

He dressed in the dark and took two cold cans of beer and two pieces of fried chicken wrapped in foil and found the man awake in his cell, sitting on the floor with his back against the wall.

"Howdy." He stepped inside. "No sleep?"

"Not much."

Chuck handed him the beers, one at a time, and the man set them on the floor at his knee.

"You never got to drink yours is what I heard."

"Thanks."

"Keep you till morning."

The man said nothing.

"Hungry?" Chuck held out the foil-wrapped chicken.

"Nah," the man said, but he took it.

"Cold?"

"I'm alright."

"Well we'll see you in a few hours then. We'll get Boyd in here and get it sorted out. Get you on your way."

"Have you seen my dog? Did someone get her?"

"Your dog?"

"I told the people in the bar."

Chuck drove around for over an hour. The man was still awake when Chuck returned at three o'clock to say he hadn't seen her. The man stared at the floor. He never touched the chicken or the beer.

Later that summer, Chuck remembered that he'd found drawings among the man's things.

"Drawings?" May raised an eyebrow and poured him another short glass of whiskey.

"Like with a pencil," he explained, setting his hat on the counter. "A woman with long hair. A dog."

"Were they any good?"

"No."

Afterward everybody assumed the man had buried the drawings with his dog, because they didn't find any on him when he turned up again.

When Chuck let the man go in the morning, he spent an hour walking around town, up and down Jefferson Street and in the narrow alley that connected the back lots of the empty stores. His shoulders were hunched inside his long, black coat, which he wore despite the growing heat. He looked even more alarming in daylight than he had in the dim bar—his skin damp with sweat, his dark hair in jagged overgrown slashes across his bony face. He returned twice to the parking lot behind the bar. He cupped his giant hands and called out a name, turning around in a full circle. He whistled up and down Jefferson Street once, then twice, indifferent to the stares from the diner.

In the night, when the man had been locked up, his dog had instinctively returned to the highway to find him. Eventually the man found her there, and he stooped on the side of the highway over the black and white fur.

Probably mistaken for a polecat, people said, black and white like that.

The man sat hunched beside the dog the rest of the morning, his head in one hand, the other on the animal's neck. John brought him a shovel. The man buried her that afternoon, and disappeared.

A huge dry storm rotated overhead that evening, howling like loose trains and beating the naked plain back to life. When the sun rose the next day, little flowers on long curling stems rose up and opened, spreading like pink smoke over the grass.

Until this particular summer, whenever Gordon wasn't with Leigh, he was with his father, and they were welding. While everyone else his age was riding bicycles, or playing Little League in Burnsville seventy miles down the highway, or later going to football games and cruising the main strip there, Gordon was being trained.

The work was a convenient excuse for what would have been inexcusable for a boy had he not been so occupied: he didn't play baseball, football, or any sport; he neither hunted nor fished; he liked to read but disliked school, and he spent most of his time with Leigh, the only other person his age in Lions, who was herself for a long time a scrappy, friendless girl with a blistering case of eczema.

The truth, however, was that he loved the work: the elegant planning and subsequent execution with the plasma cutter, the metal cutting chop saw, the oxy wrench, and especially the Precision TIG 375, which cost John Walker just about a decade's worth of discounted work to purchase. It was new the year Gordon turned fourteen, a beautiful shining red machine with a built-in water cooler, which meant he didn't have to wait for the torch to cool, mid-project. He could glide right through weld after weld, so that all the background noise of the highway, the birdsong, the radio music, and the news of the day became part of the finished joint. His father told Gordon once that in his work he must seek a precision of more than mathematical or technical accuracy, alone, and Gordon always felt he was approximating that in summer, using the TIG.

Early summer mornings in the shop were his favorite: green ribbons of prairie sandreed combing themselves through the short yellow wool of last year's grass, blue fields of new wheat. At seven o'clock he'd haul up the corrugated metal door of the shop that opened to the road, introducing a new silence, deeper than when the door had been closed. Dust motes and gold-dusted moths. Smell of coffee. Above the sheet-metal roofing, looping whistles of orioles and shrikes in the blanched sunlight. Out back his father would turn on high plains radio news. A red Dodge Ram or a long forest green Oldsmobile with shining chrome hubcabs might float past as Gordon stood in the open door. From the Gas & Grocer he might hear voices calling, a car door closing. There was the smell of sheep manure from the farms farther east. Everything moved in slow motion in clear light. He knew the days couldn't remain so. It was a sort of presentiment, a flash of knowledge in the midst of dread, the medium its very message: none of this will last.

The morning after the stranger disappeared, Gordon's father had gone north in his truck as he sometimes did for a few days at a time, and left him with two pieces of carbon steel pipe to look over. This wasn't a real job, John had said, it was just an experiment—insurance against the future. He opened his large hand on the scrap pipe. "Likely more gas and oil pipe in the next few decades, and less irrigation pipe."

"Jorgensen didn't plant any wheat," Gordon said.

John nodded. "There'll be less and less wheat."

"What do you want me to do with this?" It was much larger pipe than he was accustomed to working with.

His father had given him an odd instruction, but now Gordon had the shop door open and was doing as he'd been told. He set the pipe in the welding position, and began an imaginary weld, feeling how the electrode would need to move, how his sight lines would change continuously, how the weight distribution and position of his body would adjust themselves as he ran the bead. The line would be straight, but curved. This was difficult. Even without striking the arc, he kept losing his line. He could see why the dry run was important. He wasn't used to welding pipe this large, and even scrap like this was probably as expensive as it was rare. He stood, brushed off his pants, and turned off the radio. He took a sip of coffee, and returned to the pipe. For a moment he closed his eyes, then held the torch without bracing his arm, and again, bracing his arm.

"It's the Karate Kid," a voice said. Gordon felt his cheeks warm and turned around.

It was Dex Meredith, a big, blond, three-sport athlete from Burnsville, on his way to some college in California. He was standing beside a short guy from school, a baseball player with reddish hair. Gordon thought his name was Ryan.

"Don't let us stop you." Dex put up his hands.

Gordon walked straight toward them, reached overhead for the shop door, and pulled it shut. He stood with his back against the door.

"Sorry man," Dex called out. "You looked like the Karate Kid."

Gordon said nothing.

"He really did, didn't he?" Dex said to his buddy.

The other guy was still laughing.

"Guy is just like his dad," Dex said. Gordon could tell by his voice that they were walking away. "They even look the same."

"Got to respect him for one thing, though."

"Nope, him and Leigh haven't done it yet. Something about a family curse: welding torch for a dick."

"Shit. I would have done her in, like, seventh grade."

"I know, I know."

For the next three days, Gordon sat in the shop with the power off, the coffeepot on, and a stack of paperbacks. He knew he was disrupting a sort of ceremony of his father's—the paperbacks were to be read after work, after you'd washed your hands and eaten, and not before. But what was that rule but an arbitrary preference. After three nights, John Walker returned from the north in time for dinner.

He sat with Gordon and Georgianna at the kitchen table eating pork chops from one of Dock's hogs, sugary applesauce from a jar, and frozen peas cooked in butter. There was a little sunburn on John's cheekbones and his lips were chapped. He looked across the table at Gordon and smiled.

"The difficult thing with welding that pipe," he said, "will be the tie-ins coming into and going off the tacks."

Gordon looked out the window.

"In the morning," John said, "we'll turn up the grinder and I'll show you what to do."

Georgianna glanced at her husband and shook her head.

Gordon was aware of the sudden silence, and that his parents were waiting for him to say something, or look at them. He kept his gaze pointed out the window. "I was thinking maybe I need some time off from welding."

John looked down at his plate and cut his meat.

He did not speak again at the table, and when he was done he walked outside. Over the next four days he and Gordon would speak little, working together not at all. Georgianna followed John outside and Gordon scraped the plates and washed them, watching his parents watching the magpies.

There's one about an old homesteader with hair the color of milk poured out around her waist and knees and rippling across the hard-packed dirt floor. It's after this spirit that May Ransom named the diner on Jefferson Street. They say that Lucy Graves never leaves her house, its walls years ago regularly whitened with unslaked lime from the riverbed now dry and brown as stacked matches and surrounded by burnt gardens of splintered glass and broken farm machinery. You can find her old place north of the Gas & Grocer, back up the Monger Road and half a mile behind the coulee among the weeds.

If you're up there and pay attention—aching blue sky overhead, mute roar of eighteen wheelers on the highway behind you, minuscule flies swinging in loose knots over the tops of Queen Anne's lace—continuity stops. All time reduces to one moment, this moment, all moments the same one, this one, and there she'll be before you, plain as the hands at the ends of your arms.

All day, every day, she crochets elaborate spiderwebbed doilies of her own hair, weaving in bird feathers, seeding grasses, the shoelace tails of field mice, and tiny braids of fur from the hides of dead cattle, dead deer, and dead rats. She'll tell you about it, what brought all the settlers out and for a time trapped them on his huge, wide-open ground: misguided longing.

They told us stories, she'll tell you. And we believed them. Don't believe them. Use your eyes. Use the five good senses God gave you. Use the six.

She'll tell you they were looking for paradise, for they'd been promised nothing less. It was a story they repeated to each other so often in their journey west that even as they laid eyes on the high desert, they believed it, still. All around them, at last, a spacious country—newly cleared—in which to live as God intended men and women to live, to manifest the living Word with every pass of the plow, to amass a little of the abundance the good Lord had assured them, and to show the rest of the world what such blessings and prosperity looked like.

When it grew hot, however, and the rains stopped, the sun baked the ground. They scoured the greasewood plain and shallow rivers for as many creatures as they could find, kill, and eat. The men named their guns. The women who had lost their children named the birds and stones and missing trees, the folds of country rising up to the north into whipped peaks of dust and cracked rock.

All the while she speaks, this Lucy Graves still believes it's sometime in May 1870 and she'll politely ask for passage back home. Going west, she'll tell anyone who will listen, was a terrible mistake.

"I could be that woman," May Ransom would sometimes say to the groups of college girls passing through on their way back to the Front Range when they read the Lucy Graves story on the backs of their laminated menus. But they never asked where May was from, and they didn't need further explanation. They could see the town they had stopped in, and they could imagine living there.

The diner was a square building of white painted cinder-block, yellow curtains, and a storm door. Tiny white Christmas lights all year, white vinyl flowers glued to a green vine stapled above the front windows. A pale red-lit CAFÉ sign hanging outside.

Inside, May served fried chicken hearts, biscuits with thick yellow gravy, liver and onions, meat loaf, chicken fried steak, canned green beans, canned corn, homemade hash and mashed potatoes, coffee, juice, eggs, hotcakes, chocolate cake with lard icing, and sticky fruit and pudding pies. A thin spread of butter went on every sandwich, and she designed the most incongru-ous combinations for each: grape jelly on sliced ham; peanut butter, pickle chips, and bologna; coleslaw, cream cheese, and cucumber on grilled hamburger buns. Genius born of neces-sity, she said, since the Sysco truck came only once every four weeks—that was with even less frequency than the beer trucks brought Coors and High Life to Boyd's bar.

On this particular afternoon, Boyd sat on a swivel stool with a cold one he'd brought in from across the street, the ash-colored bruise dark on his face. The buttons on his shirt were buttoned wrong. May was behind the counter prepping for dinner, pep-pering chicken thighs laid out on two giant cookie sheets. Leigh was covering the tail end of the lunch shift and still had one woman finishing her sandwich. With every work shift, she had the increasing sense of inhabiting a reality in which she didn't seem to fit; the very edges of the counter and tables, the laminate floor, the door swinging open and closed, even the weight of her own face—it all seemed to punctuate a sense that the world was not what it seemed, not what she was relying on it to be. It was less a feeling to investigate than one to dispense with. It was a symptom of being in Lions. So as she wiped down the empty tables, waiting on the last woman, she counted and recounted her tips and added them to the growing tally she was keeping in her head, alongside the number of days until she left. There was something reassuring in the counting, itself. And when she had her totals: $788, sixty-three days, she began to amass a mental list of all the things she would get in college, where at last she'd be in the world. Sundresses. Silver jewelry. A turquoise ring. A new bedspread on a big new comfortable bed. New makeup. Fall sweaters. Boots. A real haircut.

Outside on the street, Marybeth Sharpe sat on the sidewalk in a rocking chair beside the front door of her junk store, the only such store in a string of them that was still open for business. John used to give Leigh and Gordon a dollar apiece to go inside and pick something out: a broken green dash lamp; a woman's leather boot stitched with yellowed seed pearls. A loop of steel attached to an empty husk felted with something like mold—a rabbit's foot, they determined, carried close inside someone's pocket for the most scarce and ardently sought-after resource in the county: luck. Even now, since there'd been a big snow in April, a few misty-eyed old-timers had begun to talk hopefully again of shifting rain belts. By such lights, you might still find a remote, wild, unexplored land somewhere in America, and a race of lost men living there; you might still find a city of gold, or a mountain of salt.

There was nothing remarkable about this last woman Leigh was waiting on in the diner. She must have seen the hand-painted sign for the Lucy Graves and come in off the highway, as everyone did, a constant if not thick stream of traffic from the westbound highway that kept Lions alive. She drove a silver Honda Civic, and wore white tennis shoes, blue jeans, a red T-shirt. Leigh seated her in a booth by the window. The woman ordered the lunch special, tuna melt on rye, and black coffee. She ate silently and efficiently, and set her white paper napkin folded beside her clean plate.

"Have just a minute?" she asked, when Leigh set the check facedown on the gold-flecked Formica table.

"What can I get you?"

"You're as wide open as a telephone booth."

"I'm sorry?"

"Anyone could step right in and call up whatever they wanted."

The hair went up on the back of Leigh's neck.

"You know what I'm talking about," the woman said.

Leigh glanced back at Boyd and her mother. They were bent over the counter looking at something in the Burnsville newspaper.

"Look," the woman said. "You can close the space above your head like this." She moved her small, thick hands over her own head as if she were smoothing down flower petals into a cap around the top of her skull. "Just like that. For safety."

"Safety?"

"Don't you have the sense," the woman said, "that something wants to bargain with you?"

Outside in the street the wind lifted the thin white hair off Marybeth Sharpe's head as she rocked back and forth in her old wooden chair.

"Can I get you some change?" Leigh asked.

"Tell me you don't feel it. Almost knocked me back a minute ago. What was in your head just now?"

Leigh picked up the check and looked at it without comprehending it, and set it back down.

"Isn't there anyone that you love?" the woman asked.

Without thinking, Leigh felt Gordon's hand in hers. She felt, without naming, an old song in a haunted place, a flare of heat in her chest, a key that fitted a door.

"Three seconds of your day," the woman said, again gesturing with her hands around her head. "Close it up. Do it regular. Morning and night." She took the check and began rooting around in her giant brown purse. She withdrew two five-dollar bills. "Something is already engaged." She stood and smoothed her T-shirt over the folds of her belly. "Something's in there with you already."

Leigh held the check and cash and watched the woman leave. Outside in the street the woman made a U-turn and headed back toward the frontage road. Marybeth Sharpe waved at the car from her rocking chair.

Leigh set the woman's dirty dish and cup in the bus tub, slipped the five-dollar bills into her pocket. She opened the register and closed it. Folded the woman's check and dropped it in the trash.

"What was all that about?" Boyd asked. May had corrected his buttons.

Leigh wiped her hands on her apron. "Looking for a tall man in a pair of stolen coveralls."

"Oh, shut up."

"I told her he went north, that you chased him out of town with a hatchet. She asked if you were the one who killed the dog."

Boyd threw up his hands. Over breakfast alone he'd heard ten different versions of his own complicity in various crimes involving the stranger and his dog. "I didn't kill the dog. I didn't hang it, I didn't burn it, and I didn't run it over with my truck."

"Leigh," May called from behind the counter where she was stooped with her head in the dishwasher. "Will you get Gordon or John and tell them I need someone to fix this thing again?"

"I told you I would do it."

"Don't you touch it Boyd Hardy."

He put his hands up, his beer bottle hooked between his thumb and forefinger. "Bring me another beer when you come back," he told Leigh.

May stood and looked at Boyd. "Did you give her a key to the bar?"

"No?"

"I thought I was done for the day," Leigh said.

"Go go go." May waved her hand. "But tell John we need him over here."

"I'm taking some of these sandwiches."

When Leigh reached the shop, Dock and Emery Sterling were there with John, as they often were. Emery ran across the shop in his welding helmet to greet Leigh, then walked back to the workbench stiff legged with his long sunburnt arms uplifted and flexed, the way he almost always walked, as if he were playing a game: pretend I'm stuck in a human body that can only move like this. He was always smiling, his chin wet with his own spit, and flapping his hands like big pink birds. He was the same age as Gordon and Leigh, and though in all his life he had never spoken a word, Dock and his wife Annie insisted he had a language. When from the bed he reached up to touch the ends of his mother's bright hair, that was a word. When he threw back his white-blond head and looked up at the stars that Dock told him were his cousins, that too was a word.

Emery loved the shop. He'd sit on the workbench and swing his legs in circles as he watched John show Dock how to weld the muffler bracket on Emery's ATV, or how best to attach hog wire to the steel posts around the Sterlings' lot, or how to prep steel pipe coral with phosphoric acid and water. For all of this instruction, Dock was given a small hourly wage because, John reasoned, Dock was doing most of the work himself. It wasn't charity, but it wasn't business, either. People would say John was out of his mind—he had a wife and son to support, for the love of God—and Dock, a huge man who lived modestly off his hogs and meager patch of alfalfa and whose wife had to watch their great big boy twenty-four hours a day, he, like everyone else, absolutely knew it, and was filled with equal parts wonder and gratitude. One, it seemed to him, never showed up without the other.

Late this afternoon, Dock and John were bent over a couple dozen drill tips. Dock couldn't find a drill for his no-till planter that he liked, or that fit, and wanted to make his own. That was a song John Walker loved to hear.

"You want to get them as close to 60 Rockwell C as possible," John was saying.

"Expensive?"

John shrugged. "Anything less," he nodded at the window toward the board-hard ground, "you'll be back in the shop halfway through the planting season looking for repairs or new drills."

The men raised their hands in hello as Leigh propped herself on the workbench next to Emery. "Where's Gordon?" she asked.

"In the house," Dock said.

"Two ways to heat treat the forward face of each drill," John said.

"Stick electrode," Dock tried.

"That's one," John said. "Probably the one and only instance in the world in which you want to hear the steel crack after laying a bead. But there's a second way."

"Hang on a second," Dock called to Leigh. "You want to see this."

Leigh kept her distance, but stayed in the shop to watch. John turned on the torch, lowered his helmet, and began to heat the steel. Dock lowered the shield on Emery's helmet, then lowered his own.

"Torch it till it's up to temperature," John said over the quiet roar of the torch. Emery was transfixed. The metal glowed bright red, then pale gold, then white. John turned off the torch and waited until it cooled to purple, and turned to the steel drum of water beside him.

"The faster the quench," he said, his voice deep and faraway inside his helmet as he held up the red-hot metal in the channel locks, "the harder the material." He plunged the part into the horse tank and disappeared behind a wall of steam.

Dock lifted his helmet and grinned at Leigh. "Tell you what," he said. "This old man's a wizard."

"I know it," Leigh said.

John lifted the hood on his helmet and waved at Leigh.

"I'm stealing Gordon now," she said.

"I know it, my truck too. Know what that's going to cost you?"

She crossed the smooth concrete floor and kissed John Walker on the cheek. He put his arm around her and pulled her close in a half hug.

"Bring him back," John said. "And tell him he's got work out here."

She met Gordon outside the shop beside the truck and they climbed in. The late afternoon sun picked out golden threads in the weeds around the gravel drive as he backed up and hit the frontage road.

"What were you doing inside?" she asked him.

"Watching a ball game."

"You were not."

"I was."

"What kind of ball?"

He raised an eyebrow. "Bring something to eat?"

"Got us a couple beers and sandwiches."

He touched her face. "You look good."

"*You* look good."

"Sixty-three days," she said.

"Not that you're counting."

"If I had two thousand dollars saved, I'd leave tomorrow."

"When you're there you'll wish you were here."

"Never."

"You watch." He reached over and interlaced his fingers with hers.

She rolled her eyes, and told him about the woman in the Lucy Graves. He slowed the truck and looked at her.

"Who was she?" he asked.

"Never seen her before. She had South Dakota plates. It's creeping me out. Do you ever feel like that? What she said? Like something's bargaining with you?"

"What," he said. "Like the devil?" He set his gaze back to the road and smiled.

Leigh scooted to the middle of the truck. "These things come in threes, you know."

"What things?"

She held out her forefinger. "One," she said, and pointed out the window as they passed the ground where the man had buried his dog earlier in the week. She glanced at him, then lifted her second finger. "Two, the woman at the Lucy Graves. So, what's the third thing going to be?"

"The lady today doesn't count."

"Why not?"

"Because you're the only one who knew. Besides me."

She agreed that something in the texture of it felt different.

"And if you're not sure there's a second thing," he said, "then you can't really call the first thing the first thing."

"I guess not."

"So no things coming in threes," he said. "Come back to planet Earth. Blue pickup truck." He pointed out the window beside her, and before them, the weeds and grass a pale yellow green, lavender green, and silver and lettuce and willow green, and Prussian blue and forget-me-not-blue and rose pink and gold.

"The thing is," she began, and looked at him.

"Go on," he said, "get it out."

"I don't know," she said. "It's like a tightness right here." She lifted her fingers to her chest and throat. "Anxiousness. Like there's something important I'm ignoring. But I can't place it."

Gordon stared straight ahead, not responding.

"Let's drive out to the buttes," he finally said. She studied him.

"Why weren't you welding today?"

"There have to be a hundred kinds of birds out there now."

"It's a long drive," she said, and put her arm across his neck and shoulders.

"Good. Scoot over."

It was one of a string of perfect nights, like beads threaded on a brilliant necklace that isn't yours to keep. They sat in the cab of the truck, his back against the driver's side door, her back against his chest, his arms around her. They kept the passenger side window down, and spoke little.

"Let's just sit here forever in the dark like this," he said, and tightened his grip around her waist. Outside the truck the wind shushed through the grass and lengthening weeds.

"No morning?"

"No morning."

"No evening? No factory? No school?"

"No. No nothing," he said. "Just this."

The evening slowly drifted west and shadows crept across the cool grass. Night bled into the trees. By the time they drove back around toward the outskirts of town, it was midnight. The yellow square of the Walkers' kitchen window was hovering before them.

"Were you supposed to bring the truck back earlier or something?" She thought Gordon was in trouble. The stars themselves could set their clocks by the daily routines of John and Georgianna Walker. If John was up measuring coffee in his white shirt and blue jeans, it was 5 AM and the sun was just cracking the eastern sky with a long and even white line of light. If Georgianna was rinsing greens in the sink, it was 7 PM and silver white moths were on the wing. If the downstairs lights were on at this hour, something was wrong.

Gordon dropped Leigh off first, at her house a couple hundred feet away, then circled back around, parked the truck, and went through the kitchen into the house where he found his father on the floor breathing heavily, his bare feet on top of two end pillows. His brow was furrowed. Georgianna was in her flowered nightgown on her knees beside him, her long gray hair all around her. She looked up at Gordon, her eyes streaming tears. John shifted his glance to his son. Gordon squatted beside his parents, his heart beating fast and high in his chest. Tree shadows cast by the waning moon spread black veins across the faded wallpaper roses.

There were six rules in John Walker's shop that comprised not a checklist, but a cycling number of items to be continually considered: be safe; be clean; plan ahead; check your power and connections; take care of yourself; and do the job right.

It was the first of these Gordon thought of as he drove from the clinic in Burnsville back into Lions to get a change of clothes for his mother, who'd gone in the ambulance in her nightgown while Gordon followed in the truck. The morning was the first promise of what would be a record-breaking hot summer, and under normal circumstances his father would have already been in the shop at this hour, black coffee made, in heavy work pants and a wool shirt. God, the hot days Gordon had spent as a boy in the shop dressed in boots, pants, and wool. The pitiful looks he'd cast at his father.

You can't wear cotton and weld, you can't wear polyester and weld, his father would say as Gordon flushed red and the sweat broke out in beads, a slick sheen on his upper lip and at his temples, under his arms. Set down your torch and get yourself another glass of water.

In the house Gordon gathered things for his mother: a dress, a light sweater, sandals, her toothbrush, and set them in the passenger seat of the truck. He went into the shop through the side door. No radio. No coffee. All the walls and pegboards painted white for visibility and safety were washed a pale gas blue by the early morning light. The metal of the wheels, wire brushes, cabinets, sockets, ratchets, and clamps gleamed from their ordered places. The cans of Derustit, ChemClean, and Bradford No.1 were all lined up with paint cans in the green metal corrosives cabinet. First-aid kit. Fire extinguishers, one in each corner. The old binoculars. The green and silver Stanley Thermos.

"People's lives depend upon a good weld," his father had said, and put a heavy plate of ten practice beads before him. This was some years ago. Outside it was high summer. Eighty miles down the highway every kid he knew was out in it. He watched carefully as his father drew his finger over the top of each bead, naming its flaws. "Porous," his father said, and took Gordon's finger and ran it over the top of the weld. "Incomplete fusion."

"Passed it too quickly," Gordon said.

"Could be."

"Or the current was too low."

"Exactly right."

"But these look perfect." Gordon ran his finger over the next two.

"Those are the worst," his father said. "Because you can hardly see anything's wrong. It's cracked. Lengthwise."

"And this one at the toe."

"That's right."

"This one has slag in it," Gordon said. "And here—you can tell they weren't pushing it fast enough. Look at that long motion they must have been making. An inch even. Look how wide the bead is."

"And this one?"

Gordon studied at it, and glanced up at his father. "Cracked?"

"You're guessing. Don't guess."

"Sorry."

"You're not operating from a belief system, Gordon," he said. "You're working with successive approximations of facts. Work with what you know. And what you don't know, don't guess."

"OK."

"Don't tell yourself a story about it."

"I wasn't."

"Make your own observations. Don't take my word for it—or anybody else's."

Gordon closed the shop door, his stomach clenched. It was wrong shutting the place up on a perfectly good workday. His eyes stung as he started up the truck. For the first time in his life, regret was alive in him, making his face very still, his movements wooden. He was a block past the only stop sign in town before he realized he'd driven straight through it. His thoughts went to Dex and the short baseball player, but he knew better than to assign them responsibility for the choice he'd made. Gordon had not been there for what might have been his father's last days in the shop. Days he could never have back.

He pulled over at the Lucy Graves. The lights were up and he could see May behind the counter, and Boyd, and a customer—trucker traffic from off the highway—perched on stools with small brown ceramic cups of coffee in their hands. May was frying up breakfasts as she prepped for the lunch hour. Four loaves of plastic-bagged white bread were out. Pink stacks of frozen ham, frozen salami, frozen bologna, filaments of waxed paper floating between each slice. A canister of mayo, an industrial-sized jar of bread-and-butter pickles, and ten pounds of frozen crinkle-cut french fries. On the stove behind her, several cans' worth of corned beef hash simmering in an oversized skillet. Dozens of her own hens' brown and white eggs lined up on blue dishrags beside the range.

"Gordon," May said, when he came in and rang the bells on the glass door. She dried her hands on her apron and went to him and kissed his cheek, then set her hands on his shoulders, surveying his face. "Your dad hanging in there?"

Gordon hadn't slept; his eyes were ringed with shadow. "Don't really know." He kept his gaze pointed at the floor as he spoke.

"Bad season," Boyd said to no one in particular.

"Oh, sweetheart," May said to Gordon, then furrowed her brows at Boyd to be quiet. She brought Gordon to the counter. "What can I get you guys?"

"Nothing that'll get cold, I guess," Gordon said.

"Starts cold and stays cold," she said, "coming right up." She turned around and stooped into a cooler. "Your dad eating too?"

"Just me and mom."

"You want an egg and toast while you wait?"

"No, I'm OK."

"Nonsense, let me make you an egg and toast."

"You should let her," Boyd said, "she does it really good."

She set a slice of bread over the butter and onions and cracked an egg open beside it. "Poor Georgie," she said, then she sang it again a few times, like an old song everybody knew.

In three minutes Gordon had a buttered, browned slice of toast topped with a thick slice of red tomato fried in bacon fat and an egg over easy, with a cup of black coffee. He thanked her. She glanced at the customer and then again at Boyd, both bent over dishes of peppered eggs.

"You boys set?"

"All set, ma'am," the truck driver said.

Boyd winked at her, and May gave him a stern look, shifting her eyes quickly to Gordon. She set four slices of white bread on the stainless steel counter.

"Sorry about your dad, Gordon," Boyd said.

"Thanks."

"Hell of a good man. There's anything I can do you come ask me."

"Thanks, Boyd."

"Bologna?" May asked.

"Sure."

"Jam?"

"Whatever you think best."

"Good boy," she said, opening a jar of her own chokecherry preserves.

"Tell you what, Gordon," Boyd said, and pushed his plate back. "That story of the talents. You know it?"

May went for the relish. "Boyd just tried church in Burnsville."

Gordon raised his eyebrows.

"Been a rough string of days for him."

Boyd put his hands up. "I probably won't go back though."

"Parable of the talents," the truck driver said, lifting his coffee.

Boyd looked at him. "That's right," he said, "the three talents." He turned to Gordon and explained. "Three men get a
little to go on, a little grease, right? First two guys take it and go
out into the world and get busy. Work hard. Make a little more
for the man who invested in them. Third man does nothing with
his talent. Buries it right in his hometown, never leaves. Stays
right there where all his family live and never makes any money
or does anything with himself in the world."

May snorted. "That story," she said, and waved her butter
knife, "is not about getting busy and making money."

Boyd pointed at her. "You never been to church in your
life, May Ransom."

"Responsibility," she said. "That's what it's about. You get a
little grace in this life and you're responsible for it. You cultivate
it. You keep it alive. No one else is going to do it for you."

The trucker looked at her, squinted, and frowned. "Grace
comes from God."

She peeled two pink circles of meat off a stack wrapped in
waxed paper. "Gordon knows what I mean," she said. "You learn
something in school, you don't close up your books for good.
You open another book. Right?"

"Bunch of hooey," the truck driver said, glancing up at
Gordon and lifting his coffee mug. "Your buddy here is right.
Don't get stuck in a dying town and run out of business like
your garage here." He wiped his plate with a corner of toast and
nodded toward the street.

"Levon's garage went out of business?" Gordon asked.

Boyd nodded. "He's about to. Corporate's coming up from
Denver to assess." He made scare quotes with his fingers around
the last word.

"Well, but the weld shop will never close," May said, and closed one sandwich. "Business or no business. Walkers don't care." She looked at Gordon. "Sorry Gordon."

Gordon raised his palms. "Hey," he said, and smiled, "true story."

"Chips? Slaw?"

"Yes, please."

"Hear that? Yes, please. Never hear that out of Leigh, do you?"

"Our Gordon," Boyd turned to the trucker. "So smart. He could be a doctor. His father could've been one, too."

The man looked at Gordon. "You want to be a doctor?"

Gordon shrugged.

"He's a welder," May said.

"Bet Leigh wants him to be a doctor," Boyd said.

"Good for you," the trucker said to Gordon. "Welding's good work."

"Gordon's not a welder," Boyd said. "You don't want to be a welder."

"Just don't get stuck here doing it," the trucker said.

May pushed two white paper bags into a white plastic bag and knocked a row of glasses onto the floor. She put her head down and her fingers to her temples.

"Sorry," she said. "Sorry. I'm off-kilter."

Gordon walked behind the counter. "Here," he said, and pulled out her chair. She sat as he put her coffee cup in her hand, then swept up the glass.

"I'll get out of your way," the trucker said. "Liked the eggs, ma'am," he called out in May's direction, and put a five-dollar bill, folded lengthwise, down on the counter. He put his ball cap on his head and nodded at Gordon, then Boyd. "You should go back," he said.

"What, to church?"

"'Through Him and for His name's sake, we receive grace to call people to the obedience that comes from faith.'" He tipped his hat at May, and the bells strung on the door jangled as he stepped out into the street.

"No need to go back Boyd, you just hang around the counter all day and you'll get church enough, trust me. Seems their belief grows in proportion to their disappointment. I will never understand it."

Boyd wiped his mouth and set his paper napkin on his empty plate. "That's what people get for their high expectations."

"Don't put your hand in the trash," Gordon told May. "I put the glass in there."

"I'll send Leigh over with something for dinner," she told him. "Something hot. For you and your mother."

But that was the last anyone saw of Gordon for six days.

"What do you mean he's gone?" Leigh asked at the front door. Glassy-eyed and drawn, Georgianna stepped out of the doorway onto the little concrete slab that served as a doorstep, wearing the same shirt she'd worn the day before, a small kit of some useless things for John in her hand; she was just back from the clinic. The sun was high overhead, the shadows around the two women knotted up small and tight in the grass. "Where did he go?"

Georgianna drew her lips into her mouth. She shook her head. "I don't know."

"How can you not know?"

Georgianna sat on the stone step, her shoulders slumped. She put her face in her hands. Leigh sat beside her and suddenly felt sick. Then she understood. It was John, of course. Hadn't she already known? She pulled her knees in close and lowered her head onto her arms. Her throat tightened, forcing her breath high up into her chest. John Walker, never again. Never again with his hair floating up in the wind around him. Never again with peach pie. Never again with storm windows. For a moment she had a picture of him, his back turned away from her and his body small against a rocky, white field as pocked and dusty as the surface of the moon, then she pushed it out of her mind, pulled a chain and the lights came up and she was in the diner serving fried potatoes and hot black coffee and bright yellow eggs, saving her tips. Fifty-seven days, $812.

A breeze rattled the metal screen door behind them. In the high grass and weeds across the dirt road, red-winged blackbirds looped against the blue sky. By early August, the heat would drive all the birds away, and the Queen Anne's lace would shrivel in the sun. The white phlox would never bloom at all, and half the town would be gone, and all the old folks, and the last of the children. It was as if Gordon and John had taken all the familiar world with them that day they left.

Boyd and May pulled up in his big, black pickup and May rushed from the cab to Georgianna and embraced her. Boyd walked across the yard with his head hanging.

Don't make any sense, they said in town.

That man was healthy as could be.

And young. What was he, fifty-five?

Came out of nowhere and took him.

Good things happen to good people, they said, and shook their heads.

He was irresponsible, they said.

Stubborn.

Backward.

Never saw him in church.

Kept his family in poverty.

Boy's the same way.

He'd best take this as a sign.

All night Leigh stayed awake with the light on, turning over the shiny, perfumed pages of a magazine. If she drifted off, John was greeting her in the shop, setting a cold hand on her upper arm and smiling, and asking for a sandwich, and what had she been reading? He could recommend a good cowboy book about true love and good men and mystery, but it was going to cost her.

When she was six and seven and eight, and home alone while May ran the diner, Leigh would cross the yard between her house and the Walkers' and crouch in the grass when the front room was lit, and watch the three of them gathered together, Georgianna and Gordon playing gin rummy or blackjack on the braided rug, and John in his reading chair with his small glass of whiskey on the end table beside him and some old paperback open in his clean, calloused hands. Sometimes, one of them heard her out there, and John or Georgianna would bring her in, and after cards and cocoa put her to bed on the floor in Gordon's room, in his favorite G.I. Joe sleeping bag, covered with the orange and brown living-room afghan. Then sometime just before dawn, John would carry her like a doll in his arms back to her own house. On some of those mornings, she lay in bed and heard John start his truck and drive away, and the truck would be gone for days in a row. When he came back he'd point without a word at his cheek and she'd rush to give him a kiss, and they'd all go together to the diner for dinner. Mashed potatoes and gravy, canned string beans, sugar pie.

"Where'd you go?" she'd ask.

"Looking for gold."

"Did you find some?"

"Mountains of it, and guess what? It doubles when you give it away."

"Can I have some?" she'd put out her hand and he'd snatch it, and she'd squeal, laughing.

"That's the catch, Miss Ransom. You can't ask for it."

One night, two, then three nights and still no Gordon. Outside the Lucy Graves the earth shimmered. New crab apples baked on their branches and fell like stones. A yellow dish of lawn circled the base of each tree. At night in the distance, across the road and a flat pan of dirt so hard it glittered, heat lightning flared. By day it was ninety-nine, then a hundred, then a hundred and six degrees. Ragged cowbirds perched on the rusting spools of fence wire. The house windows and metal gutters blazed. It was still only June.

Leigh ran her fingers through her hair. Drank a Coke at the empty lunch counter, looking out across the empty street. Pressed the cold, sweating glass to her cheek, then inside her skirt, against her thigh. Across the street a stiff, hot wind moved the fingers of a dead cottonwood against a sky so blue it made the backs of her eyeballs ache.

She couldn't bear a whole summer of this. So hot, so bored. So angry she could feel her heart beating in her forehead.

She turned restlessly on the stool toward the kitchen and saw John on the pale, empty moonscape. She turned the other way, toward the street, and saw Gordon walking up behind him.

The sun was too bright. Her stomach hurt. Summer was terrible. Lions was terrible. Her whole life she'd hated it, and

Gordon loved it. She knew he did. He was the worst. And she knew exactly where he was, she could see it all. Eventually he'd tell her, too, because he told her everything. Right in line with John's directions, Gordon would've started the old Silverado, left the clinic right after John finished talking, and followed an unpaved county road that cut exactly north between the Altons' field to the west and the Jorgensens' to the east.

Leigh knew the road. They'd been on it together. It was so seldom used that for miles at a time it narrowed into a single lane, disappeared in the weeds altogether, and appeared again like a faint line of chalk drawn through the BLM land littered with white primroses, prickly pear, and cow shit. Gordon would follow it all the way up. He'd drive until the roadsides were crusted with dirty ice, and woofs of snow blew off the tops of the mountains in the distance. It was an arid, rocky country, with naked gray bluffs of stone and small fists of sage and scrappy trees like upended bits of frayed twine. When the road passed between two uplifted planes of granite, he'd slow the truck, look back, then accelerate and speed through.

For hours, no matter how far he'd drive, the horizon would appear no closer, and look no different, unless for a moment it was marked by the dots of ragged horses out to pasture. A scarf of smoke rising in the vacant blue. An abandoned kitchen range, its siding chewed to a rustwork of lace. As he checked the road ahead, the rearview, then the side mirror, shifting his gaze in a triangle of points, he'd see a shadow racing around, just ahead of his vision, like an intuition that's there, and gone. Daylight receding beyond the ridge to the west as he sped north, and from the east a band of darkness slowly closing over him like a lid.

"It's not just you facing this thing," John would've told him. "It's you and everyone who came before you."

Eventually in the years to come, after two trips north herself searching for him, or for Boggs, whomever she might find first, Leigh would come to understand it all.

How fast the landscape changes when you pass Horses up there, then Three Bells. How the wind sings and moans like an old song you can neither place nor stand to hear. How Gordon wouldn't have been able to get the picture of his father in a hospital bed out of his mind. How all he'd have thought about was how good life had been, and how it was supposed to have gone.

He'd stay at the North Star that night, a motel planted in the middle of nowhere with an American flag, the whole place pinned to the dirt by a metal pole topped with a neon-green star that rocked in the wind. Inside the motel, the carpet a filthy off-white, smeared with greasy stains. Coffee burnt in its glass globe on a little brown Formica counter beside a basket of bruised, red apples. He'd call out a hello, but nobody would come. He'd ring the rusted silver bell on the desk. Still, no one would come. In truth he'd be afraid of who might respond. There'd be no other cars in the lot of sloping, cracked asphalt. All of the room keys—nine of them—would be hanging on red plastic diamonds behind the desk. He'd take number three because it was Leigh's lucky number, and go back out and around to the room. One soft gray tennis shoe at a time, he'd decide right then to leave cash and strip the bed himself in the morning.

Despite the strangeness and sadness of the circumstances, he'd make a civilized time of it in that motel room—Gordon was like that—arranging his things, settling in. Double bed with a heavy green blanket and two windows that looked out over a flat field of blanched dirt and pale grass whipped by the wind into matted blond whorls. The wind would be huge outside but the room warm and the bed firm and comfortable. He'd fall asleep as soon as he crawled in, and dream the dreams of stones. Morning, and everything it would entail, could wait.

"Let me make you some tea," Georgianna said, and stood up at the table.

"No, no," May stepped farther into the house and closed the kitchen door behind her. "Don't move. And tell me where you keep the honey."

Georgianna sat back down and pointed to the cabinet beside the sink.

"Did you sleep last night?"

Georgianna rubbed her face and nodded.

"Lipton good?"

"That's all there is."

Both women had red eyes. May brought over cups and tea bags.

"Was he peaceful, Georgie?"

Georgianna looked at May, then back to the table. "Very peaceful, yes."

"Was he aware of you?" May asked.

"I crawled up in bed with him. Then he was gone." She turned to the space beside her and touched the open air. "I had my head right there on his chest, where I'd always fall asleep. Every night since we were twenty."

May's eyes filled again. She took her old friend's hands in her own. "He went easy, then, right beside you."

Georgianna nodded, mouthed yes.

"Do you know where Gordon is?" May asked.

"Yes and no." Georgianna took a ragged tissue from her pocket and touched it beneath each nostril.

"When he'll be back?"

"Couple days I'm sure."

"We're not going to leave you alone until he's back."

"Oh, I'm OK."

"And don't you worry about the memorial or funeral—me and Dock and Boyd will take care of it. You just direct us, OK?"

"Thank you, May."

"Do you know what John wanted?"

She shook her head.

"We'll wait for Gordon."

May watched her. They'd hand-stitched yellow and blue–checked cloth napkins together for their kitchen tables when they were twenty-three. Quilted for their babies when they were both pregnant, those quilts now faded and soft in Leigh's and Gordon's bedrooms. They'd shared preserves and chicken casserole recipes, been drunk, been furious, been fine.

"And now the children will leave, won't they?" Georgianna gazed out the window over the yard and toward the weedy fields.

"I'm afraid so."

"I wish they wouldn't."

"I know it, honey."

"Maybe they can stay. Run everything for us."

May laughed. "We'll put little paper umbrellas in our drinks and put our feet up. Can you imagine?"

"Yes, and then they can go, later. Some other time." They both laughed. "May," Georgianna said. "It's going to break my heart. Both of them at once. All of them at once."

"The kids aren't dying. And I'll be right next door."

"I don't believe Gordon will go," Georgianna said. "I don't. He has work here. His father. You know how they are. How they were. How John was."

"Sweetie. Lions isn't like it was even six months ago. And it's always been bad. There's no business for Gordon."

"I know it."

"Hardly anyone comes."

"I know."

"You think it's temporary. Is that right?"

"There've been times like this. Seven years once when John's grandfather didn't have a single customer. Seven years."

"I don't know how they got by."

"They got by."

"Did he leave you anything? Life insurance?"

Georgianna shook her head.

"Damn it, John," May said.

Georgianna opened the tissue and blew her nose, crumpled it back into a ball.

"Maybe you can come work in the diner finally, huh? Been trying to get you in there for years. Employees eat free, you know."

"I'll make my city chicken."

"From Omaha."

"And my cousin Julie's corn soufflé."

"Yes."

"I didn't think it would be so soon."

"I know, honey."

"It's so quiet here now. No one makes a sound."

"People will be coming by, now."

"They will?"

"Of course they will."

"I feel sick."

"I'll go to Burnsville tomorrow. Get you ginger ale and whatever else you need. Let's make a list."

"He was almost out of Lava soap."

"First item."

Just before ten, after sitting with Georgianna until she drifted off, May found three men at the bar. Chuck Garcia, Dock Sterling, and Erik Jorgensen had quietly taken their places. Boyd had the television off. They could see clearly across the street into the diner, where Leigh sat alone at a table with a melted milkshake and an untouched grilled cheese.

"She's been sitting there since dinner," May said. "Poor kid."

"John was like her dad," Boyd said.

May gave him a look. "I should have been so lucky."

Boyd glanced up at her sharply and Dock and Chuck laughed.

"She must be sick about it," Dock said. "That and Gordon."

For a few minutes, no one spoke. They could feel the weight of the news between their shoulders. John Walker, gone. They lifted their drinks, eyes fixed in the middle distance.

"It doesn't bode well," Boyd finally said. "Boy leaving as his father's dying."

"It does seem a little irresponsible," Chuck said. "Not like Gordon."

"Aw, give him a break," May said. "How many of you sat still to watch your own fathers die?"

At the end of the bar, Jorgensen cleared his throat. The old man had dressed up to come into town, as he always did, in a stiff white-collared shirt and a wool vest and ironed Wranglers. His thick, white hair was as bright as a flare in the dim bar. "Never saw that boy without his dad," he said, his hands trembling around his beer. "Followed John around like a shadow."

That wasn't natural either, they said.

No young man felt that way about his own father.

Makes you wonder what's wrong with the boy.

"It'd be work," Dock said. "I'm sure that's where Gordon's gone. They have customers all over the county."

Boyd made a sound in his nose. "Customers? Around here? No disrespect," he said, "but I don't understand what all of John's work was for. I mean no offense." He shook his head.

No one said anything. Dock stared at the black window, dark as film. Jorgensen gripped the bar.

Boyd went on. "Guy from some big fabrication plant in Chicago passed through couple three years ago driving his kid out to college. Said he'd never seen work like John's, and he didn't even have the most up-to-date gear. Said John could have started at a hundred thousand a year in Denver, easy. Aerospace. Military. Hell. Lots of natural gas pipeline getting started up in Wyoming."

"Heck, Boyd," Dock said gently. No one really had to explain. John Walker never invested a goal—like finishing a harrowing frame or hog kennel—with the power to give purpose to his day, let alone meaning to his life. Rather, everything he encountered, each drill, each small project, was itself his life for the duration of the project. His was not the work of a man who believed in or even thought about the future. He looked ahead only as each project required planning, even as he worked on the task at hand with a kind of myopic ceremony.

"Five hours he'd have me at rust removal on a piece of steel no larger than my hand," Dock said, and lifted and opened his huge white hand.

"Maybe he was autistic," Boyd said.

"That's an ignorant remark," Dock said.

"Sorry. Sorry, Dock."

"How was Georgie when you left her, May?" Chuck asked.

"Sleeping in one of his shirts, in his old chair. I invited her to come stay with us, but often as not our house is empty too."

"What they should call this place," Jorgensen said, staring straight ahead at the shelves of bottles. "Empty. Whole God-blessed place." He broke *blessed* into two syllables. "I can't remember ever seeing this town anything other than empty. The past was great, they said. The future will be great, they said." He gave them a look of wonder. "None of it was true."

They all grew quiet. Everything was heavy. Their beer glasses. The boots at the ends of their feet. Their own hands.

"You know what I think it is with Gordon," Boyd said, picking up Dock's empty. Boyd grabbed a clean pint glass and pulled another and set it in front of Dock. "Come on," he said. "You're all thinking the same thing."

"Oh, shit," Chuck said. He drained his own beer and set

the glass on the inside of the bar. "There's no Boggs any more than there's a Lucy Graves."

"Listen," Boyd said. "Everyone chose that first Walker to get the dead guy out of town and take care of it. And then his son, and his son's son, and his son's son's son."

May handed Chuck a new beer. "Last one for me, Maybelline," he said.

"He was an Indian," Dock said. "Right?"

Chuck shook his head. "You guys are always seeing Indians where there are none, and never see the ones who actually live around here."

"Name like Boggs?" Boyd ignored Chuck. "He was a trader. He was visiting the territory, and got trampled, or shot. Supposed to have a tombstone somewhere out here. Homesteaders' cemetery maybe. Have you ever seen it?" he asked Chuck.

"Not me."

"You're all idiots," May said. "This is the real world, hello." She knocked on the bar. "There is no Boggs, and Gordon is off grieving somewhere."

Boyd ignored her. He rubbed his mustache. "So the Walkers picked up the sick guy. Or the dead guy, whatever. Forced to tend him what, five generations? Bring him firewood, blankets, canned food. Maybe, hey," he raised his glass, "couple beers now and then. And starting this week, it's Gordon's turn."

"It's why they never leave," Dock said.

"And they could have. I've heard John has a hundred thousand dollars saved that he never spent."

"Not true," Chuck said. "Me and Emily just bought Georgie's groceries. He didn't leave her a thousand dollars. Where would he get the money? No one paid him for his work."

"People only owe us what we imagine they'll give us," Dock said. There was a silence. "My father used to say that."

Boyd pulled another beer for himself. "And what happens," he went on, "if the Walkers stop? If no one takes care of the guy?"

Chuck pointed his beer at Boyd. "Maybe the task falls to you, Boyd."

"Hell, I'm not taking care of any dead guy. Someone holds the town together by keeping the demon out, it's not going to be me."

"Anyway, poor Georgie. Somebody's going to have to look after her."

Chuck looked at Dock. "You got to make Gordon go," he said. "He'll be wanting to stay. He'll feel like he has to."

"Oh, he'll go," Boyd said. "He won't let that girl head off into the world without him."

"Gordon will never leave," Jorgensen said, staring at the label on his beer bottle. They all looked down the bar at the old man. "It's an interesting story," he said, "for a town like this. In times such as these."

"What, Boggs?"

Jorgensen raised the bottle and drank, then set his empty on the bar. "But the next man I hear associating that kind of garbage with John Walker and his family, I'm going to break his nose."

Boyd's face grew hot. "Beg your pardon, Mr. Jorgensen."

"Heck," Jorgensen said, "don't beg mine."

May went down to where the old man was sitting and took the empty bottle. "You want another one?"

He raised his hand. "Not for me."

"We see you didn't plant any wheat," she said. The men watched her. "I heard Mrs. Jorgensen wants to go."

The old man nodded.

"What are you going to do?"

"Know how Dorrie and I have managed fifty-one years of marriage?"

"How's that?" May asked. Everyone was listening.

"Two words: Yes, dear."

The men laughed.

"Minot, I heard. Is Dewayne there?"

"He and Lisa have an extra room."

"Well, Mr. Jorgensen," Chuck said. "We'll be sorry to see you go."

"Well." The old man stood, his blue eyes rimmed with red, and looked at each of them in turn. "I can make more leasing my water rights than I can growing wheat," he said. "There's just too damn much surplus. And too little water. Tell me, how do you figure that?"

Dock made a sound of affirmation.

Jorgensen shook his head. "Here's another riddle for you," he said. "How long can a man believe he lives in a country that doesn't actually exist, standing in the middle of one that does?"

"Oh, come on now," May said. "Is it as bad as that?"

"Seventy-one years at least. And I've known older men and women than that around here. Seventy-one years telling myself it's farm country. Or that it's this or that kind of country." He shook his head again. "When you finally wake up," he said, "it's too late. You're an old man." He opened his hands, trembling before him.

"Where would you have gone?" Dock asked him.

"Might have just adapted to what's actually here. That would've been the most sensible thing."

"Surprised to hear you say that," Chuck said.

The old man grinned. "Doesn't sound very interesting, does it?"

"Well, come on," Boyd said. "A man wants to make something of himself."

"The endless becoming," the old man said to that. "You become a farmer. You become a businessman. You become a Christian. You become a Democrat. You become a Republican. To hell with it all." They were all quiet a moment, then Jorgensen raised his hand in farewell. "Well, anyway," he said, and pushed out through the door. His old Ford pickup was in the street. They watched it pull away.

"God," Boyd said, "people work themselves to death around here."

"Perhaps you all didn't know it," May said, "isolated out here as you are, but the point is no longer to work hard. It's to survive the longest, and the most comfortably."

Chuck whistled and picked up his hat. "Go easy on us, May."

May reached back and turned up the lights. "That's it, men," she said. "Go home and get some sleep."

It was by their happiness that the good people of Lions approximated their value in the eyes of the Lord and, if you asked them, they would tell you how happy they were. How blessed. On Sundays most of them drove to the Bible Church in Burnsville, so while Lions was small enough, and bare enough, Sunday mornings it was dead empty, and absolutely still. In early summer, as on this particular morning, if you went out walking over one of the weedy fields or even down the dusty road toward the highway, the plain would open for you, pretty as a prayer book. The last of the white stars faded and the day slowly absorbed the paper face of the moon, like a soft blue cloth soaking up a small white spill. Georgianna Walker woke alone, and moved through the rooms of the house, opening windows, then stepped outside toward the highway.

She was in her tennis shoes and nightgown when Chuck found her walking along the bar ditch. He pulled over slowly behind her, a good hundred yards behind, and hustled to catch up with her on foot. He didn't want to startle her.

"Mrs. Walker?" he called as he jogged, his keys jangling. It was a warm day already, the deep greens from snowmelt and early rain already drying out. She did not stop. She was carrying a white wooden cross. It struck him as odd. There were crosses like that stabbed into the front lawns of some of the houses across Lions, but he didn't remember ever having seen one at the Walkers' place. The Walkers weren't like that. "Mrs. Walker! Georgie!" She paused and looked back. Her pale eyes were radiantly blue. She smiled, and he fell into step beside her.

"Making me run, at this hour!"

"I'm sorry, Chuck. I didn't know you were there."

"Good morning, Georgie. Are you in your nightgown?"

"Oh," she said, with a little embarrassed laugh, "I figured everyone was in Burnsville."

"Now didn't you say last night when we left you that you'd take good care of yourself?"

"I'm sure I did."

"You shouldn't be alone on the side of the road like this."

"Oh, Chuck I'm OK. And I'm hardly alone," she said, and put her hand on his arm. It was worn and wrinkled and lined with veins. "But thank you."

"What have you got there?"

She held it up. The cross was six inches wide and ten inches long. "We had it in the shop," she said. "I don't know what on earth for, but now of course I'm glad we did."

"What's it for?"

"For the dog, Chuck," she said. "We meant to do it right away, but John got sick."

He was quiet a moment. "Can I help you with it?"

"I'd appreciate the company and the help."

They walked side by side until they came to the place where the grass had been overturned and the man had placed a small cairn of stones and gravel. Around them the long fingers of morning light played in the grass, fascinated with it, teasing and combing it in the wind. Georgianna sat down beside the pile of stones in her nightgown and set a hand over it.

"Poor creature," she said.

An old pickup with a handmade wooden trailer sped past, rattling rusted metal.

"So loyal," she said, "you know?" She looked up at him.

"Good dogs are that way."

"We could have all up and left the town but if this dog thought that man was still here somewhere it would've waited forever."

"It's a strange thing."

"Beautiful thing."

They kneeled over the little mound and just above it dug at the dirt and gravel with their fingers until they had five or six inches cleared out.

"Should've brought a spade."

"Oh well," he said, "now we have dirty hands from good work."

She smiled. "That sounds like John." She placed the cross upright and held it still while he filled in the dirt. Then she sat back down in the dirt and held out her hand, palm up. At first he didn't know what she was doing. Then he sat beside her and took her fingers.

Chuck could see she was crying, and his eyes filled with tears and he pulled his lips into his mouth.

"We are so sorry," she finally said. "Forgive us. Amen."

"Amen."

A rig filled with sheep sped past and stank horribly. Instinctively Chuck held his breath in his nose for a few seconds after it passed. Georgianna brushed off her nightgown and stood, leaning on his hand to steady herself.

"Will you join me and Emily for supper later?"

"Thank you, Chuck, but no. I'll gladly take the ride home though."

"Absolutely. Don't you move. You wait right here and I'll pull up the car."

Every day was brighter and hotter than the day before. The air hung still around the empty blocks of Jefferson Street. Hot wind pulsed in the open windows. The highway rippled in dusty waves in the distance. After five days, still no Gordon. Chuck considered filing an official report but was swayed by Georgianna, who said she knew where Gordon was—just taking a break from the world, John used to do it regular—and that he was fine.

For some of the old-timers, disappearances like Gordon's were just part of living in such deceptively wide-open country. Any of them at the Evening Primrose nursing home could tell you about a handful of faces they'd known as children, and you don't see them for years, and then there they are again, those old faces at once bright and familiar and ravaged with age.

They'd show up at the bar, maybe.

Or they'd be right there at the nursing home in lawn chairs propped up on the grass with blankets over their laps.

Went off looking for something, some said to explain it, but came back.

Gone forever, others said. Joined that old procession of ghosts walking back and forth, back and forth, from the West Wind motel on the far edge of town and out across the howling wilderness, people and their dogs and mules and covered wagons and broke-down Chevrolets all rolling slowly over the chalk hills and through arroyos beneath a haze of sparkling dust.

It'd started in the hours before dawn one summer some four hundred years earlier when a tribe of men, women, and children left the Spanish colony in New Mexico where they'd toiled beneath the desert sun, and left in pursuit, it's said, of freedom. Imagine rows of squash cultivated in the midst of alien flowers blooming on cactus. Oxcarts lined up in rows. One sprawling, low-lying adobe fort and half a dozen shacks and outbuildings. Silent as a herd of cats, a band of families, natives and Spanish, French and Mexican, gathered at the edge of the outpost where patches of hard corn met the sand, and left. Quietly walking, no running, no horses, to the north and east. They crossed over a thousand miles, one step at a time, an entire people gone overnight, as if kidnapped. The Spanish, alongside the French, led by a blue-eyed, black-haired man who'd had his nose bitten off in a fight, sent out their own search expedition to find them. These missing people had been their property, it was said. On horseback they combed the plains from present-day Mexico up through Arizona and New Mexico, and ended up right around Lions, on the high plains in eastern Colorado, before all tracks ran out and the search party turned around empty-handed.

It was said by witnesses—men hauling furs and liquor across the Southwest on mules or in ox-drawn carts—that they vanished in broad daylight, and that their number increased all the time as new wanderers joined them.

Truckers have seen them.

One guy who runs I-80 from eastern Iowa to Reno will call it in twice a year. A thousand of them, he'll say, their hair blowing back, kids, mules, white men, red men, black men, yellow men, women of all shapes and sizes, baskets on their heads, packs on their backs. And you don't want them to look at you, he'll say. You don't know why but you don't.

Marybeth Sharpe once claimed to have walked among them for an hour one afternoon, from the old Dairy Queen to way out behind the northernmost edge of Jorgensen's hay fields where bluffs from the dry riverbed begin to rise up into the mesa.

They have no particular aims or goals, no ambition, neither hope nor regret. Over the years, they've pulled others into their circle. Children, men, women, lost or mistreated animals. Anyone out of place—anyone who notices when, say, a single white star aligns with a stone peak and a blue spruce. If you're attentive, you'll see it. If you miss it—the painted doorway, the odd gentleman, the woman who seems to be looking up at you from deep within a well—they'll disappear, and the gate will close again.

"Let me in," Gordon would sometimes try, addressing, say, the evening star.

"Gordon, no." Leigh would come up behind him, his face pointed out the broken window at the stripe of cottonwoods waving their hands in the twilight.

By the morning of Leigh's eighteenth birthday the red potted petunias outside the Lucy Graves had shriveled into black tissue paper, like spiders on stems, and the gulls and terns that used to inhabit the standing water of irrigated fields until mid-summer had already left for the landfill south of town.

Leigh watched the window for the Walkers' truck—he wouldn't forget today. Now he would come. By lunch when the volunteer firefighters led by Chuck Garcia passed the diner, it was already one hundred and three degrees. Chuck's lights were spinning, but no sirens.

"What's this?" May leaned out over the counter. "There a fire?"

"Anything moving that fast on a day like this is heading toward a water hole," Boyd said, and as it turned out, he was right.

Leigh stepped into the street, and he and May followed. There were three customers in the booths, all strangers from the highway, and they stayed where they were.

Marybeth Sharpe stood up from her rocking chair in front of her store, and waved.

"What the heck's going on?" Boyd called to her.

"Search me," she hollered. She was grinning, her wide hips jutting out from the top of a wide, long, dark skirt. Something was happening—it was like a holiday.

Still in her apron, Leigh went with Boyd in his truck. They passed the Evening Primrose where an ambulance had already stopped. Stricken faces of nurse aides and old folks hung like white ghosts in the heat. Boyd slowed and followed Chuck's vehicle.

Behind them, May hustled the last of her lunch patrons, turned the diner's "open" sign to "closed," crossed the street, unlocked the side door to the bar, and sat in the cool dark to wait.

By the time Boyd and Leigh reached the source of the commotion, the first responders had already emptied out of the firetruck and begun the systematic process of opening the water tower. It took Chuck and his assistants very little time to figure out the trouble, because a similar thing had happened recently in Chicago, where a young man had been murdered and his body dumped in the water tower on top of an exclusive hotel. The Burnsville ambulances filled up with five sick children from the day care and eleven old men and women from the Evening Primrose before heading back toward the clinic. Diarrhea, vomiting, crippling stomach cramps—and knowing what'd caused it made everybody sicker. They found the tall stranger in the tank of the town's water tower—his lungs full, his abdomen bloated, his coat spread open like black wings—floating just beneath the surface in his liquid tomb. Chuck and the men from Burnsville tried to keep the people of Lions back, but they all crowded around fifty feet from the tower, where Chuck had set up tape. Then, of course, they all turned away, hands over their mouths—even the grown men. Boyd held Leigh up on his arm and brought her back to the truck.

When they returned, Boyd joined May in the bar, which he decided not to open that night. He poured a whiskey, then sat beside her.

"Did you hear?" he asked her.

"You better tell me."

He told her. She sat staring, her face propped on her hand, her hand over her mouth. "His face was all—" Boyd's voice roughened. "It was terrible, May. He was coming apart."

"Did Leigh see?"

Boyd nodded.

"Ah, shit. Where is she now?"

"Waiting for Gordon somewhere, I'd say."

Boyd and May sat with their elbows on the bar, their drinks between their hands.

"If that boy's gone another day we ought to have Chuck do something," May said. "Send someone after him."

"Georgianna doesn't seem worried."

"I'm not sure she's got all her faculties about her. You should see her, Boyd."

"I've seen all the seeing I can handle." He emptied his glass and poured another.

"I knew it was bad," she said. "And our fault."

"Aw, come on, May," he paused and looked at her over the rim of his glass. "We don't know why he did what he did."

"Why are you drinking whiskey, then? In the middle of the day?"

When children in Burnsville told it, the stranger was still alive when they found him, and he choked out his last watery breath right there in front of the three men and one woman in coveralls who came from Burnsville to drain the tank. They said that days earlier, a man with a big silver mustache had led the people of Lions, who carried the stranger above their heads and down the street and dumped him in the water tower with their own hands. They said the stranger was hard to kill, that he fought for his life. They huddled together in the bathroom in the dark and looked into their own reflections to see the fear that was in his eyes when the cone-shaped lid was lowered down over him.

But in Lions, no one—not the children, not anyone— wanted to talk about it. And no one wanted the tank, which had been there since 1919, cleaned or refilled. The county coroner came out for the body, and Chuck put out a wire, and made that call to North Platte after all. There was no record of any missing man from the place or from any town nearby who fit the description and, in fact, no record of any missing man fitting that description in decades' worth of records.

"Not like we'd know if he'd been missing for years," the representative from Nebraska told Chuck on the phone. "But you do sometimes hear a story like that."

"What about before that?" Boyd asked Chuck later that week. "Like, you know, a hundred years back?"

May set her hand on Chuck's shoulder as she passed behind him with two cold beers on a tray. "Don't encourage him, Chuck."

Chuck didn't think it was funny. He'd dropped the ball. He should have taken a photo. Wired out the details. Put all the information in the bank. He should not have visited the man in the night and brought him beer. He should not have booked him informally, or at all. The dog, the man, all the people sick, it was his fault, in a very real and legal sense. He wondered why everybody blamed Boyd instead of blaming him. It was a whole godforsaken county of ardent belief and powerful imagination; he couldn't always tell which they were guided by, or whether there was much difference between the two.

On the night they found the body in the water tower, Leigh stepped over the dull metal guardrail on the frontage road and over the same loose wire the man had crossed some few weeks before. She held her breath as she neared the Walkers' house. The old orange reading lamp was lit over John's chair. She half closed her eyes and looked at the living room window through a blur of eyelashes, then let herself in through the back door. Georgianna was alone in the kitchen in John's giant slippers and a long workshirt that came down past her knees.

"Oh," she said, "come in, dear. Come in, oh you brought us pie."

"Rhubarb," Leigh said. She set the Styrofoam carrier on the counter. "From Edie's garden. But I only brought two slices."

"You have Gordon's," Georgianna whispered. "I won't tell him."

"Is he back?"

Georgianna smiled at Leigh. "He'll be back. Don't worry. Would you like some tea?" Georgianna set the kettle in the sink to fill it. "That goes good with pie, right?"

"It's so hot out, though."

She went on filling the kettle.

"Georgie, did you hear what happened?"

Georgianna turned the faucet off and faced Leigh. "It's terrible," she said, opening her arms and folding Leigh in. "My poor husband. He's died."

Leigh started, then relaxed in the woman's familiar hug.

"I keep looking for him."

"Your shirt smells like him," Leigh said. The same Lava soap Gordon used. The same deodorant. Almost the same sweat.

"I don't want to wash it."

"You don't have to."

They stood there in the kitchen, holding hands, sweating, swaying. The ceiling fan whirred overhead. Leigh could smell the sweet, cheap White Shoulders perfume from the Walgreens in Burnsville that Georgianna had worn as long as she could remember. The feel of Georgianna's hands, soft and old. All of it knit up into a memory Leigh would push out of her mind in the years ahead, a moment of communion in a kitchen as familiar as her own, with a woman as familiar as her own mother. Georgianna put her hands on Leigh's shoulders and surveyed her face. "What else do you want to eat? I have meat loaf, tuna casserole, a sheet of lasagna, macaroni and cheese, peas and corn, Jell-O."

"Oh my God," Leigh laughed. "Who brought you all this stuff?"

"Everybody."

"We should call Boyd and Dock."

"Bring 'em over. Bring the boy too."

"Can I call them?"

"Call them up. We'll have a birthday party. You got to have something, right?"

So Dock and Annie and Emery came over in their truck and they all sat outside in the grass beneath the cottonwood and ate cold meat loaf and pan-fried lasagna and Jell-O.

"They have their own well, don't they?" Annie asked Leigh in a hushed voice as they were gathering up dishes and carrying the pans outside.

Leigh nodded.

"It's horrible," Annie whispered, leaning in. "Dock's really spooked."

Leigh nodded, eyes glazed.

But for Emery, whom Dock took to the shop to retrieve his helmet, they were all quiet as they ate. Annie poured them sticky, pink wine from a gallon bottle. The breeze was warm and Dock made a cheerful fire in a ring of stones. Emery roasted marshmallows, howling from inside the helmet at the flames and swinging the burning sugar around in bright red and yellow circles in the dark. The weedy yard was alive with firelight.

"Summertime," Dock said.

"Emery and fire," Annie said. She poured Leigh another plastic cup full of wine and refilled her own. "Who else wants more?" Annie raised the jug.

"That stuff is awful," Dock said, and extended his empty cup. "Fill me up. Where's that boy of yours, Leigh?" He nudged her with his shoulder. "It's his best girl's birthday, for Pete's sake."

"He's fine," Georgianna said. "He's camping." She shook her head, smiling. "Lions, population a hundred seventeen. Too crowded for the Walker boys."

Dock caught Leigh's eye, and she glanced back at him with a look of fear. At least, that's what he told everyone in town.

If Gordon was going up there to see someone, they said, he would've told her.

If he didn't tell Leigh, he wouldn't tell anyone.

"Well, happy birthday, anyway," Annie said, and they raised their plastic cups.

"Happy birthday, precious daughter." Georgianna smiled wide. "Three pieces of advice for our new adult," she said.

Dock took a sip of the sweet wine, then tipped his head back, consulting the stars. "Here's one I learned from John." He glanced at Georgianna. "Four words you need to ask yourself every day: what if I'm wrong?"

They'd heard John say it before.

"Oh yes," Annie said. "That's a good one. My turn?" She

touched her fingers to her chest and Leigh nodded. "Advice for our new adult. Here you go." She looked into her cup, then turned to Leigh. "Never have more than two drinks?"

Dock laughed. "Is that a question?"

"Two?" Leigh said. "This is my second already!"

"Cut her off, people," Dock said.

"Georgie, your turn." Annie nudged her.

"Oh, dear," Georgianna said. "This was my idea, wasn't it?"

They waited. She scanned the horizon with a faint smile on her closed lips, then settled her gaze on Leigh. "Don't go anywhere," she finally said.

"Don't go anywhere?" Leigh smiled, not understanding. She wasn't going to die, if that's what Georgie meant.

"Stay with us."

"Aw, come on," Dock said, "that's not fair." He shook an index finger at Leigh. "Don't you listen to that."

"Gordon won't go," Georgianna said. "Not now."

They all looked at each other.

"So you ought to stay with us," Georgianna said.

Stay in Lions? It was unthinkable. It was not only bare, but cursed, the whole county comprised of no more than searing light and eddying dust. Nothing but wind and white sun. It seemed even you weren't there. It seemed you were standing nowhere, on nothing. No ground. And there was no future in Lions. No matter how many stories you heard about years gone by, no matter how many plans you had stocked up for the future, you were confined to a never-ending present.

Dock flashed his eyes at Leigh. Emery plunged his stick through the heart of another marshmallow and torched it, spinning fire in spirals in the darkness behind them.

"What if," Georgianna said, and blinked at Leigh, "what if you just stayed?"

Leigh shook her head. No one could stay sane and remain in this place of stillness, emptiness, and unbearable light.

Georgianna shrugged and smiled. "My advice," she said.

Of all its haunts, one of the scariest place in Lions was Echo Station, named after a children's game featuring an abandoned gas station on the far west end of town where giant weeds had cracked up the concrete and spread the broken pieces apart like a clay dish shattered against the hard ground.

It hadn't been a large gas station, just a single bay wide enough to pull in and lift a single car, and a small, glass-cased room with a register and cooler, and a toilet behind a small door. The glass had long since been broken, and there'd been nothing in the place in recent days but a single piece of bent rebar pointing like a bony finger right at the doorway, where you'd stand looking in. The gas station had been built on the same site as an old sod stagecoach station of a hundred years before, which had later been chosen as the spot for Lions' railroad station. There'd been tremendous hope that the railroad would be directed through Lions. It would have enlivened the town and brought all kinds of people and quality products and services everyone missed from back east. Burnsville, however, was chosen instead. So even when the gas station was new, it was felt sharply as a place of disappointment. Add to this that the gas station didn't last a single year—a town the size of Lions didn't need two, and the Gas & Grocer had bread and canned food and fresh milk. Given the chance, the people of Lions might have excised it from their maps of town. It was a symbol of regret, of bad decisions, of misplaced hope.

After its owners left for Denver, the station was looted and for years stood empty and open to the elements. It ate all the sleet and rain and sun and wind, and seemed when you passed by to want to suck you in, as well. First, children in the backseats of their parents' cars took to holding their breath when they passed it. Then they began visiting the place on foot, in twos and threes, the way people in a larger city might go to have their palms read, or fortunes told.

You were supposed to stand before the empty gas station alone—your friends had to wait a good hundred feet off—then close your eyes, make three counterclockwise circles, count backward from twelve, and open your eyes. Immediately in the space before you, the dust and light would take the form of either a past or future self who had some kind of directive. This could be a single word, an image, a feeling, or the name of a distant city. It might be the shape of something, like a key or an apple or a door that you would have to look for in your life as a sign by which to get your bearings. But as you stood there before the whirling dust at Echo Station, you wouldn't be able to tell if you were being guided by a self who was young and full of wishes, or old and full of wisdom—so the sign could lead you to a life either of peace and abundance or of poverty and bitter sorrow. Once you put your faith in Echo Station, however, and closed your eyes and turned three circles, it was too late. Your fate was sealed, the direction fixed.

It was a game that had almost passed out of knowledge by the time Leigh and Gordon were kids in Lions, and it was Dock who told them about it. They were at the diner eating ice cream and pie one summer night, and Annie had just taken Emery to the bathroom. Boyd was new in town that summer and up at the counter talking to May, who kept smoothing her hair and smiling.

"We wanted a ghost story," Gordon said when Dock told him and Leigh about the game. "That's not a ghost."

"I don't know," Dock said. "Scary enough for me. I wouldn't play it, that's for sure."

"Really?" Leigh asked. She licked her spoon. "You never did?"

"Nope," Dock said. "Never have, never will. Grown-ups know better than to go looking into the abyss. Besides. Don't I already know how my life turned out?"

"Scaredy-cat," Leigh said.

"You bet I am."

"Let's do it, Gordon," Leigh said.

Gordon put his napkin on his empty plate. "No," he said slowly. "I think I'm with Dock."

"Come on."

"I don't get it, anyway," he said. "You won't even know if you'll get rich and happy or sad and poor. You'll just know that you've made it stick."

"That's right, Gordon," Dock said, and pointed at him. "Don't even play that game."

Gordon crossed his arms and smiled and repeated it to Leigh. "Don't even play it."

That night Leigh walked alone through town in her nightgown and tennis shoes, and stood among weeds almost shoulder high, and closed her eyes, and made three circles in the dark. On her way home, smiling, she stooped in the middle of the road and drew a heart in the dust with her finger.

Gordon woke at home in his room in early evening, sunlight leaping like copper-colored flames among the tree leaves outside. Smell of toast and coffee from the kitchen below. The clatter of cookware. He couldn't have said what day it was, or how long he'd slept, but when he sat up straight his mind felt sharp. Outside the window, a shimmer of dandelion floss. The dry fields creaked. He could hear them.

Down the hall and stairwell, the wall clock, the framed wedding stills of his parents, grandparents, and great-grandparents, even a very blurry, grim image of his great-great-grandparents in white ballooning clothes that looked as though they'd been fashioned from boat sails, and each of the smooth wooden steps, the flowers and stripes of the wallpaper—it was all looking out at him.

"Grief wakes you up," his father had once said, talking of the loss of his own father. "You might not want it to, but it does."

Now there was nowhere to hide. That Gordon had ever taken comfort from such things. From moonlight on the sidewalk. From wind in the trees. From familiar silverware, or cloth-bound covers of old books, or the faces and gestures of those he loved. The longer he looked at these things in the days to come, the more familiar and simultaneously puzzling they seemed.

He put his hand to his head and went down the steps while all around him, the nail heads and floorboards announced that they were no longer simply what they appeared to be, though they were quite clearly nothing but nail heads and floorboards.

Downstairs, the front door was open. Outside the air was still hot from the day and smelled of the Sterlings' small hog lot. Only late June and the clump grasses were already blond. Bindweed and vetch curled and spread themselves in a purple tangle over the ground. A warm wind bent the line of young alders John had planted, and sheets and thin, white tea towels billowed and leapt on Georgianna's clothesline like long parallelograms of pale blue light.

Georgianna was sitting in John's old chair with one small, heavy glass of whiskey beside her. His reading lamp cast a circle of yellow around her in the dim room, but her face was chalky. She was not reading but looking into the middle distance, like a woman under a spell.

John's routine after work always went like this: washing his face and scrubbing his hands with Lava soap, then coming down for supper, and performing a little ceremony Gordon watched with great interest as a boy. In the cabinet just over the silverware drawer, where Georgianna kept measuring cups, an old red and black cardboard check box filled with rubber bands and paper clips, and an old, smooth, bent horseshoe, there were two heavy shot glasses, with one teardrop of air inside the bottom of each. Sometimes, Gordon would go into the kitchen and take them out of the cabinet and weigh them in his hand. Cool and heavy, like magnifying glasses. His father would fill them each up to the top with whiskey, and drink one standing there by the sink, all in one motion.

The second small glass he would carry to his chair, lamp, and bookshelf, which were situated beside the woodstove but facing the window, out toward the frontage road, as if he were on watch at the end of each day. When Gordon realized, as a boy, that this was what his father's habit brought to mind, he was both worried and curious about the adversaries his father seemed to await every single evening of their lives.

"Nothing I'm expecting," John told him, "which is why I'm paying such close attention."

Here, at his chair and table, John would set down his second glass and clean his eyeglasses with a soft, faded yellow cloth, turn on the lamp, pick up his book from the night before or open a new one, and sip the second shot as he read.

"Rejoined the living, I see," Georgianna said to Gordon now, with a smile. "You must be hungry."

Gordon stared. The wind from outside filled Georgianna's white curtains with moving light. Behind them, the shapes of trees, hedges. Next door May's Barred Rocks and Rhode Island Reds clucked and screamed.

"He passed almost right after you left, Gordon," Georgianna said. She lifted the whiskey, and sniffed it. "I can't believe he drank this stuff."

"How long have I been asleep?"

"Long time. Leigh's in the kitchen."

He sat down. "Can I—" He looked outside again, then back to his mother. "Can I still see him?"

"If you want to. He's in Burnsville. We've been waiting on you."

Gordon nodded. "I'm sorry."

She waved her hand. Reached for a tissue.

"Has Leigh been here all day?"

"Just this hour. Everyone's helping out."

They were quiet a long time. Georgianna cried and Gordon stood to hand her another tissue. She took it and balled it up in her hand. He looked toward the kitchen door. He could see Leigh's back, the knot of his mother's apron tied around her waist. He turned back to his mother just as Leigh turned away from the kitchen counter and stepped closer to the doorway to listen.

"Was it—was he—"

"Peaceful," she said, and nodded into her tissue. "Just fell into a deeper sleep. Hardly made a movement."

Gordon struggled for a moment, and got it out in a whisper. "I couldn't watch."

"I know."

"Did he say anything?"

She shook her head. "It's like he was already gone. You saw him."

They were quiet another minute.

"Mom," Gordon said. "Did you and Dad ever talk about going back to Lincoln? With your parents?"

"Back to Nebraska?" She set down the whiskey and folded her hands in her lap. "Your dad's work was here. You know that. And after Grandma and Grandpa died there was no reason to go back."

"But you could have moved the shop."

"Yes, we could have moved the shop."

"He would have done well in a bigger city."

"He certainly could have."

"And wouldn't it have been better for you?"

"Better? For me?" She shook her head. "I don't know, Gordon. Why?" Then she smiled. "You're trying to imagine what kind of woman might want to spend her life in Lions, and why."

He shrugged. "I guess that's right."

"You've been traveling."

"Traveling?"

"Your father always called it traveling. And he always came back so serious. So sharp. Ready to work."

Gordon leaned forward, his elbows on his knees, and half covered his face with his hands.

"I won't ask you to talk about it," she said. "I know that's sort of against the rules, isn't it?"

He smiled a little. Ran his sleeve beneath his nose. "I guess so."

"He doesn't begrudge those last days, Gordon. I know he doesn't."

"I'll never forgive myself."

"Don't ever say such a thing."

"It's like my whole life I've been climbing a mountain," he said, "and when I was up there, and knew he was gone, I could see."

"What could you see?"

His eyes filled with tears and again his throat closed up. He spoke in a hoarse whisper. "Everything." He pressed the insides of his thumbs to his eyes and felt his lower lip and chin begin to tremble. "And now," he said. His voice cracked. Georgianna waited. It came out again in a whisper. "Now I'm coming down the other side."

"Tell me one thing," she said, "so that I know. In case I need you. Which direction do you go?"

Gordon's eyes touched hers.

"Tell me," she said.

"North."

"Same place."

"Yes."

"OK."

"You know where it is?"

"Of course I do."

Where she stood listening in the doorway, Leigh's knees went weak. She couldn't hear any more of it. She turned from the door and crossed the kitchen slowly, her knees unsteady, her stomach unsteady, and went back to the counter where she lifted a cool, raw egg and held it in her hand. She looked out at the yard, and down at the egg, then cracked it into Georgianna's mixing bowl. Two, three, four more, and she whipped them into a pale yellow foam.

In the living room Georgianna lifted and sniffed the whiskey again. "I didn't marry your father as a way to get nice things, or to be confident that we'd be living a certain way," she said. "Love is not about comfort or consolation, Gordon. Is that what you wanted to ask?"

"Maybe," he said.

"You want to ask me if your father was crazy."

"No."

"It's OK," she said. "It won't be the first time someone's asked me. But I can't answer it for you."

He nodded.

"And Gordon, even if he was, it doesn't mean you are. You don't have to keep the shop. You don't have to spend your free days up north. You don't."

He looked at her. He thought her hair was whiter. He'd never realized how much she resembled his father—the shape of the eyes, the long, even ridge of the nose, the wide cheekbones. Gordon had heard say of people who live side by side for many years that the cells and even atoms of their bodies begin to align with each other's. Eventually they not only cease to look like themselves but begin to resemble each other. So what happens when one of the two of those people disappears?

She patted his hand. "It's exhausting," she said, as if she could hear his thoughts.

Years after this summer Leigh consulted a doctor about grief and hallucination, about grief and heartbreak. She was in Denver at the time, and found herself wandering around a pretty, green park that was, it turned out, a hospital grounds. There was a statue of St. Francis in the middle of a fountain ringed with flowers of stone, their crenellated petals sparkling with mineral glitter. She sat beside them at a bench beneath an alder and was soon joined by a physician eating his lunch out of a brown paper bag. He was old, soft around the middle, with iron gray hair and brown eyes. She imagined he had an old wife at home who had assembled this lunch, with sliced apples and a flat whole-wheat sandwich cut into four triangles, as if he were a child. They greeted each other, Dr. Saunders, his name tag said, and when he finished a triangle of his sandwich, Leigh asked if she might trouble him with a question.

"A medical question?"

"Of sorts."

"Are you a patient here?"

"No."

"Have family here?"

"I'm just waiting for someone."

"I'll try to answer it for you," the doctor said.

She articulated the question as best she could.

"Ah," he said, and smiled a little sadly at her. "Dying beside your one true love and passing into the eternal together. The stuff of legends."

"Can't a person die of grief?"

He smiled and shook his head. "I've never heard of any such diagnosis."

No doubt the old doctor believed he was making a helpful statement, but it sounded to Leigh like words from a man who'd never really loved anyone. Even an actuary—a mathematician—could tell you that a grieving person can be distraught, distracted, self-destructive; that there is, in fact, no place in the body where grief might not make its home.

"What about grief that makes you hear things?"

"Like voices?" He looked at her curiously.

"And see things."

"Visual hallucinations, too?"

She looked out across the green. It was impossibly bright. "Where you imagine whole worlds," she said.

He frowned. "Imagine, or see them?"

"Where it seems like," she shrugged, "like you believe in unbelievable stuff."

"It can be a lot of stress." He looked up into the blinding blue sky above him. "I lost my wife, for instance."

"I'm so sorry," she told him, and she inadvertently glanced at his sliced apples.

"I live with my daughter," he said. "Every morning, one lunch for my grandson, one for me."

"That's a nice thing."

"That kind of stress can do a lot of harm," he continued. He was looking at Leigh steadily now. "For a while, for a year even, you maybe really fall apart. I've seen that. That's normal."

"A year, even?"

"We all have our turn at loss, eventually. Then we understand the need to be patient."

She stood. "Thank you. I'm so sorry about your wife."

"Look," he said. He half stood, as well, and caught his lunch in his lap and sat again. "It's not my specialty. You should ask someone in the field. Would you like to talk to someone? Would you like a name?"

"I'm from out of town."

"Well. OK. But do talk to someone in the field."

She pictured the old ground behind their ruined houses, tiny, lace-winged insects glittering above the feathers of weeds.

In the Walkers' kitchen Leigh set a cast-iron skillet of steaming eggs and a plate of buttered toast on the wood table by the window. She was afraid to look at Gordon. Afraid of what he'd seen. Afraid of what she might see in him, now.

Yes, everyone agreed, the boy changed that week. In town they remarked on it—his transformation, the striking resemblance to his father when Gordon lost a few pounds, when the sun had drawn lines around his eyes and across his forehead. Even after his first visit, his features seemed sharper. His gaze, sharper. He was sunburnt, and gave Leigh the impression of having visibly aged. He would not meet her eyes, which she took to mean he didn't want to talk about any of it: where he was, what he'd seen, or what was now required of him. Suddenly she saw herself at the head of Georgianna's table, in Georgianna's apron, holding one of Georgianna's wooden spoons.

"I've got to go," she said. Gordon stared directly at her from across the room.

"You won't stay and eat?" Georgianna asked.

"Can't." She raised a hand in farewell, or hello, and turned to the back door.

Georgianna went on setting the table for three.

When they lowered John Walker into the ground, Gordon took his mother's hand. The chaplain from the Burnsville funeral home read a psalm and blessed the assembly, and gave thanks for the day. Slowly, one and two at a time, those in attendance turned away toward their cars. Georgianna and Gordon stood fixed at John's side.

"Gordon," Leigh said softly, and touched the back of his shirt, but he did not move or speak.

"Boy's heart is broken," Dock said, taking Leigh's arm in his own. His own big blue eyes were red and full of tears. "His mama's too. Give him time."

They drove in a line to the Walkers' yard, which smelled like grilled meat, beer, baked sage, and mosquito repellent. Leigh watched Georgianna turn from the kitchen sink when Gordon walked in barefoot in his blue jeans and take his face with both her hands. The screen door was propped open by an old red brick. May was setting up card tables, and Dock was grilling. It was a long, barrel-shaped grill John and Gordon had welded with expanded steel.

Together, Gordon and Georgianna stepped outside. Faces materialized out of the greenish gold light and looked at them, eyes bright in their heads, lips drawn. There was old Wade Till's sad, equine head.

"Gas station," the old man told Gordon. "You going to stay, you going to need to serve the people passing through on their way to somewhere else. Gas station. Coffee shop. Good quick hot food. What kind of food do people like," he wanted to know, "and what kind of coffee? People your age," the old man said. "What do they want?"

"I don't know, Mr. Till. You'd have to ask them."

"But we don't have any!" another old man interjected, watery brown eyes, fine purple veins cracked beneath his pale cheeks. "You see the problem we're up against?"

Emery Sterling's wide smiling face. His laughter ringing through the solemn, hushed stands of two and three men and women holding paper plates of hamburger and macaroni and pork and beans, his laughter spiking around a murmur of macroeconomic and agribusiness and slow death and bullshit and what to do, how it is, nothing more to say. So many faces in the greenish, tea-colored afternoon, this garish light the preface to a storm that never came. Grainy faces peering out at Gordon as if from old photographs, stepping right out of the print, dead people closing in around him, their eyes stony, their mouths hard, thin lines, their faces so stern. Everyone old, everyone poor, everyone white.

And their hands. Ragged, blue-veined hands. Spotted hands. Hands reaching out to take Gordon's, and touch his shoulder, and take his elbow, his forearm.

"Here," one of them said, and led Gordon to the front yard. Across the dirt road, two ruts in the ground made by wagon

wheels, made by a 1932 International truck, made again, perhaps, by a 1983 Chevy. The faint lines of dirt tracks disappearing
in the distance like a road erasing itself in the weeds.

"I want you to take a look at that," the old man said. "You
see that?"

Gordon nodded.

"You know who comes next to a place like this? If anybody
comes next?"

Gordon looked at his face floating in the heat.

"Recreationalists," he said. "Or nobody. You a recrea-
tionalist?"

"No, sir."

"You a birdwatcher? You think backpackers and birdwatch-
ers need a welder?"

"Not likely, sir."

"Think nobody needs a welder?"

"Sir?"

"Go to school."

"Yes, sir."

"Finance."

"OK."

"You got to think of the future."

"Yes, sir."

"Eventually you got to start making some money."

"OK."

The old man's bright eyes narrowed and peered at him.
"You think I'm wrong?"

The hand of an elderly woman led Gordon to a card table
draped with a blue paper tablecloth and piled with sandwiches

and warm foil trays of food. She showed Gordon where the plates were.

"You're as skinny as a snake," her face said. It wore pink lipstick. It had yellow teeth. "You fill up a plate."

"Yes, ma'am."

"That's good. Put some chicken on there. Macaroni. Good." She named all of it. Corn. Jell-O salad. Deviled egg. The paper plate was a flat, warm, shimmering blob. "Beans," she said, "good. You like hot sauce?" She shook a thin pool of neon orange beside his macaroni.

The plate tipped rust-colored bean sauce on his light blue shirt. Little white macaroni bones in the grass. Voices around Gordon saying no incentive. Junk shop. Saying yoked.

Their faces saying sad man.

Saying north country.

High country.

Saying that boy? Gordon?

Pretty girl.

Cross to bear.

Goddammed shop.

Worthless ground.

Big promises.

Some garden.

Rats and weeds.

The busy whisper of rumor and wind shushed through the trees as the barometric pressure began to drop and the hair rose on everybody's arms and necks. Georgianna stood across the yard looking pale, soft, vibrating at a low, even undetectable frequency. She wore her light green dress, the color of June Grass, her hair the color of the pewter sky behind her, as she floated from one neighbor to the next. Gracious. Empty. Invisible against the curtain of the green and gray world.

She was amazed by the number of people who had turned out, people from Greeley and Sterling, from as far west as Ault and Severance, everyone who knew John and respected him and had enlisted his work. Her old neighbors and friends stood around her, uncomfortable in the heat, imagining where they would go next, not only in the days ahead, but after the meal, and later that night. Next hour, next day, next city, next world. Apologizing in every other breath for her husband being gone, as if their continued existence somehow made them culpable for the death of one among them. But isn't it written that God is close to the crushed in spirit? And so what is knowing God but having known and lost a tremendous love? And what is knowing a tremendous love but seeing it everywhere, in everything, at all times?

They ate and ate and ate in that terrible heat. They felt but did not speak of the man in the tower. They opened cans of Coke and 7-Up and Country Time lemonade and beer but they didn't touch the water.

May set out a molded aspic of hard-boiled eggs and diced ham. They ate the glistening, savory jelly off Styrofoam plates. Dock mindlessly grilled three packages of hot dogs until there was nothing left but blackened husks. The clouds evaporated and a blinding white sun burned through a royal blue sky and the din of the creaking fields grew all around Gordon. That others could hear the sound, he was certain, for each old man and woman, when left for a moment alone on the scabby lawn beneath that searing daylight, would tip his head, and stare off into the distance where dust coiled like smoke above the weeds, right where his mother had fixed her own gaze, as if suddenly attuned to a low, pervasive hum.

"It's just the sound of the highway," Leigh said.

Gordon turned and searched her face. He looked down at the hand she'd placed on his forearm, and back up to her eyes.

"Poor son of a bitch," Levon, who owned the garage, said, standing a few feet away. "Begging Georgianna's pardon," he said. Then Levon looked at Leigh, his mouth twisted up in a sorry, half smile. "Don't hitch yourself to that wagon, sweetheart," he said.

Gordon gently withdrew his arm and stepped away.

Levon shrugged. "What?" he said, his hands up, palms open, deflecting blame. "Apple don't fall too far from the tree is all I'm saying."

"They may be old and they may be ugly but they're right about most of it," Boyd told Leigh as she approached the cooler set up in the shade of the giant old cottonwood. "College is the only way out of this hole," he said. "Go be a lawyer. Make a pot of money."

"I am."

"I have no doubt. You and el Gordo."

"Pft." She gave Boyd a look.

"You should follow him up there, Leigh. Maybe it's a spell like in a fairy tale, and the Walkers have been waiting for a beautiful princess to rescue them from the terrible Boggs." He waved his fingers in the air as he said the old pioneer's name.

"I am not a princess."

"Or maybe," Boyd said, "maybe it isn't Boggs at all he's seeing. Maybe it's a woman. A whole bunch of them."

She rolled her eyes at him and stooped to open the cooler. "Women?"

"Haven't you heard of that cemetery up north? Stretches in a long line across the grassland north of Horses?"

She stood with a green bottle of beer dripping melted ice through her fingers. Boyd eyed it, raised his eyebrows, and took the cap off for her with his key chain. "What cemetery?" she asked, and took a sip.

It was discovered, he said, when a group of students from her future college were surveying the grounds outside of town and found a series of faint stains in the dirt, each separated by about a mile, like a barely perceptible broken line down the middle of a wide dirt highway. Beneath each mark, the remains of a woman or a girl, all of them buried in dresses, striped robes, sheepskin blankets, and European boots, and hide slippers and beaded moccasins, even a pair of tennis shoes. Whatever the journey, whatever the trek, the women and children were always the slowest, so they were always the first killed by whoever pursued them from behind, and often as not, they were the only ones killed. Whatever the goal of travel—the next ridge, a hunt, a seam of gold—it always cost something. The so-called graveyard that these archaeology students found stretched some six hundred miles long, by exactly the width of a single woman or girl.

"They just buried them and moved on?"

"Gotta keep up," Boyd said. "Stay with the head of the pack."

"What shit."

He raised his hand. "True story. Look it up in the library when you get to school."

Leigh looked away. "So every woman was traveling the same path over all those years? Through Horses?"

He shrugged. "Maybe it's wider than a single line of bodies. Maybe there's girls and women buried everywhere." With the toe of his boot he opened the cooler and nodded at it. She stooped and took out another for him. Across the Walkers' backyard on the brittle yellow grass old women were hugging each other and men shaking hands, saying their goodbyes.

"You know we're just messing with you, Leigh," Boyd said. "Gordon's a good man. You stick with him."

"You and your shit stories," she said, and took a long pull off her beer.

"That was good," he said. "You timed that just right, the jibe and the drink. You'll be real nice decoration in a bar when you grow up."

"Takes one to know one."

"Come on," he said. "Don't you want to move into John and Georgie's house? Or no, wait, maybe Gordon will build you a nice little Quonset hut, right off the Quonset hut."

She closed her eyes a moment. "Leave me alone, Boyd."

"Don't believe it about John having saved a hundred thousand dollars, either. Walkers don't have five bucks between them. Careful with the beer."

"I'm fine."

Faces of the old white men and women began to pull away, then the cars pulled away, U-turning slowly and heavily on the dirt and gravel road, heading back toward town and back toward the vast dried-up farms to the east and south.

May covered the leftover sandwiches and Leigh took down the card tables. Annie and Dock brought Emery into the house where he clutched a grape jelly sandwich that dribbled down his yellow Snoopy T-shirt and Georgianna put him in front of the television and found cartoons, unrecognizable cartoons of blocky uninteresting squares and triangles in a blank yard, and she and the Sterlings talked about taking over the shop.

Gordon went looking for Leigh in the kitchen, but found May. "Leigh went to the diner," May told him.

"I thought it was closed."

"She brought back the pitchers and plates."

"By herself?"

May set her gloved hands down in the suds and looked at Gordon. "You got to forgive her, Gordon."

"Forgive her for what?"

She paused, and picked up a casserole pan. "She's not as smart or as pretty as she thinks she is."

"Leigh?"

"She's got just enough of each to make all the wrong decisions," May said, then she turned up the old AM/FM radio with her damp and sudsy pinky finger.

On the narrow back road that cut through the darkening weeds, Gordon took his father's truck into town and pulled up to the single lighted window of the Lucy Graves, closed for the day. Inside, Dex Meredith was holding Leigh in a half-slumped dance across the linoleum floor. The jukebox was lit up. There was an electric candle at one table. A white ceramic coffee mug. An open bottle of Boyd's Four Roses. The light in the diner cast a perfect upside-down image of the bottle floating in space outside the truck windshield.

Gordon turned down the headlights, pulled around the corner, parked, and came into the diner quietly through the back.

Dex saw him immediately. "I told her to slow down."

Leigh turned, disentangled herself.

Gordon looked at her. At Dex. "Let's go home, Leigh."

"I'm sorry man," Dex said. His button-up shirt was pressed, his blond hair gelled into place. His shoulders were wide; he was a big guy, but Gordon was taller.

"She filled up a whole mug," Dex said. "I tried to stop her. She's really drunk. She's really upset. About your dad I think." He lowered his voice. "She saw that guy in the water tower. Did she tell you that?"

Gordon said nothing.

"She says she wants me to marry her," Dex said.

"Is that what she said?"

Leigh giggled and put her hands over her face. Her makeup was smeared. Gordon put his arm around her and turned her toward the door. Dex grabbed Gordon's wrist and Gordon jerked back but Dex had him. He dropped three wrinkled ten-dollar bills in Gordon's hand.

"She was trying to buy from me."

"Buy what?"

"I won't sell to her. I won't even give it to her, dude."

Gordon took the money and put it in Leigh's pocket.

"I didn't touch her, man," Dex said. "Everyone knows she's yours. Not that I wouldn't want to. No offense."

Gordon said nothing.

"I'm sorry about the other day. I'm sorry about your dad. My dad liked him. Whatever people say."

On the way to Gordon's truck Leigh twisted out of his arm.

"I can walk fine," she said, and tripped over an unlevel lip of sidewalk. Gordon gathered her up again and she let him. He opened the passenger door and buckled her in, and rolled down the window. She closed her eyes and leaned back. They drove out of town in silence. Once he pulled over for her to vomit. He walked her into the house and May stood and turned off the television.

"Oh Christ, Leigh," she said. "Gordon, you OK?" She took Leigh on her arm and squeezed Gordon's hand.

Next door Georgianna was awake, still dressed, sitting in John's old chair, her hair down and all around her like a cobweb, an untouched shot glass full of whiskey on the table beside her. In the dim light, a faint line of hair across her upper lip.

"I keep looking for him," she said. "I don't understand where he's gone."

"Come on. Up to bed."

"You know, don't you? You know where to find him."

"No, Ma."

"Would you tell me if you did?"

"I'd take you with me. Straight to him."

"Are you leaving again?"

"Maybe in a few days."

"It's hard to be here, isn't it?"

When she was asleep in his bed, he went outside and across the lawn into the shop. He left the lights off and walked slowly around the room. He could barely lift a hand to touch the old radio dial. The old coffee machine. He sat down beside the TIG thinking he would never move again. Didn't need to, didn't want to. He sat still, breathing calmly, then went into the back room for an old wool blanket, and unrolled it on the concrete floor and set his head in his arms.

In the days ahead Gordon was attentive to his mother and polite with May and Boyd. He fixed the diner dishwasher and he drove south of Burnsville with Boyd where they helped butcher a steer and brought the meat home wrapped and labeled for the freezer at the Lucy Graves. He helped the Jorgensens pack and separate what they would bring to North Dakota from what they would sell or donate to the Goodwill in Burnsville, and he filled the bed of his truck six times and drove there and back to make the donations himself, for which he was rewarded with fried chicken and frosted white cake. He was twice as quiet as usual.

Like his father.

In all the ways.

Kid his age.

Leigh won't put up with it long.

I think those two have busted up already.

Shame.

Better for her in the long run.

"You and Gordon have a lover's quarrel?" May asked late one afternoon. She handed Leigh a spray bottle of bleach and water.

Leigh walked out from behind the counter toward the empty tables. "He's not the same."

Then May told her, as if Leigh didn't know, that Gordon's father had died. She looked at Leigh seriously, as if she were trying to communicate something gravely important, her pale blue eyes as steady as Leigh had ever seen them. "Leigh," she said. "John Walker is gone."

"I know," Leigh said.

"Say it back to me."

But Leigh wouldn't say it. In the first place, why? How stupid and embarrassing. And in the second place, that wasn't how they talked.

Gordon was particularly kind to Emery and Marybeth Sharpe, and Leigh noticed it was somewhat odd that she should pair Gordon with these two. Gordon and Emery in the Sterlings' front yard, the only time Leigh ever saw Gordon play ball, Emery's wild throw fast enough to knock the teeth out of your head. Marybeth coming into the diner with a crooked old finger pointed up and a faded postcard in her hand to show Gordon.

Another day, May put a scoop of ice cream in a dish for Gordon, and Leigh watched him carry it to Marybeth and squat down on the sidewalk beside her rocking chair. Gordon had come in and out of the diner without speaking to Leigh. Outside, he squinted in the sunlight and smiled up at Marybeth.

Leigh looked out across the street from behind the lunch counter as the two sat quiet on the sidewalk in the blasting heat. "What do you think those two talk about?" Boyd asked her, handing her his empty coffee cup for a refill.

Leigh shrugged. She took the mug and filled it from the half pot behind her.

Boyd nodded. "She's an odd one."

"So is he."

"More and more," he said.

"Do you get the sense he's being so nice to everyone to make a point?"

"What point would that be?"

"Something about me."

He looked at her and smiled. "Yeah," he said. "I don't think so."

Outside Marybeth touched Gordon's arm with her palsied hand, and wrapped her fingers around it. The blue irises in her eyes seemed to be dissolving into their whites, and her hairline was every year receding farther back from her spotted pink forehead. "You never go to church on Sundays," she said.

He laughed lightly. "Can't say I do."

"Your father never did."

"No."

"He traded all he had in this world for the three kingdoms." She opened her trembling hand and counted off on her fingers. "The one, the two, and the three."

Gordon looked up the street to a small tornado of dust. "Which three are those, Marybeth?"

In response she gripped his arm tighter. The ice cream was melting into a bright pink soup in the little white dish. "Gordon," she said, "you are such a good boy."

"Oh, I don't know about that."

"I do. There's some of us that do."

"OK."

At dawn in his mother's kitchen the following day he filled a paper grocery bag with canned goods, the labels bright and cheerful: ranchero beans; cling peaches in heavy syrup; chicken and dumpling soup; beans and canned spaghetti. He took a flat can of sardines, and a plastic-wrapped roll of paper towels, and a sack of red apples. From his closet he took a wool blanket, his old G.I. Joe sleeping bag. From his father's bookshelf, he took a dozen old cowboy books, an illustrated copy of *Aesop's Fables*, and a world atlas. When he stepped outside in his blue jeans, the sky was still a soft black. He started the truck and took the narrow county road up north.

Nothing like raising crops on the high plains, Jorgensen used to say, for the spiritual workout of reconciling what you'd expected with what you ended up getting. The place was uninhabitable, too hard, too dusty, too dry, too poor, out of jobs, out of prospects. The wonder was that they had all stayed so long. For years, like a slowly lifting line of birds there'd been a steady, gradual flight out of town. Finally, in this single summer, all but eleven people would go. One at a time in the old brick stores and painted houses the windows were boarded or punched out with stones, eyes blind to a place so many had years ago shed so much blood to claim.

Not until now did the hangers-on allow themselves to consider the real possibility of larger, cleaner houses, of rooms filled with light, of backyard gardens that grew more than bitter turnips, bitter greens, and woody radishes. If the minutes and hours of the day were meant to be filled with industry and improvement, if people were meant by their own toil to increase the abundance with which they'd been blessed, and if indeed God helped those who helped themselves, then life was not meant to be lived in Lions. They ticked it off on their fingers. The drought and heat and emptiness were not so life-threatening as they'd been generations ago, but were still discomforts they had no real cause to endure.

They'd been driving to Burnsville for school, for church, and for groceries for years. They cared little or nothing for this land, which rendered them nothing. From within their small, dusty houses they made plans. They talked it over with each other. They called their banks. They called the real estate agents or a schoolteacher or a bartender they knew and made plans for a new life in Burnsville. It was like laying up treasure in heaven. So did most everyone remaining in town come to see themselves at the center of a story of redemption. Somehow the country had been lost to them, and now they would reclaim it. Chuck Garcia, who had chosen Lions as his home base in the county for its quiet and expansiveness, was amazed by this sudden activity and conviction—even in his own house.

"We can't stay," his wife said, looking back over her shoulder, holding a folded, coffee-stained doily. "You know we can't."

"Why can't we?"

"Besides. It's Burnsville."

"Since when is Burnsville everybody's answer to everything?"

"There's actually stuff to do there, for one."

"Things to spend money on."

"And so what? Anyway I want a garden."

"You want a garden. It's only forty miles away, Emily. It's the same altitude. Maybe a little higher. The same dirt. You think it'll be so different?"

"Yes," she said, and resumed folding napkins and sheets. "Edie knows a woman who has three raised beds in her backyard and feeds her family off that all summer. Tomatoes, squash, eggplant. Gets lettuce straight through October."

"What does she water all that with?"

"In Burnsville they have the reservoir."

Life there would be a lot like life in heaven. A number of saved among them were being transported to a newer, better place where everyone would conduct themselves more honorably and get along with each other and in general be much more satisified. Time moved chronologically in accordance with the unfolding of a divine plan. All of this felt right. Leaving felt right.

"Jesus tells you to leave your house and your home," their minister reminded them in Burnsville. "These are his words, my friend. Not mine. 'Leave the dead to bury their dead,' he says.

"Do not be bound together with unbelievers. For what partnership have righteousness and lawlessness, or what fellowship has light with darkness? We've all heard about the man in Lions this summer. Not a coincidence, my friends, but a calling out from the Lord Himself to which we are compelled to respond. Do not hesitate to find and protect your own sacred space from evil. Easy? Of course not. Are you attached to the world? Are you attached to the little things and ways of your life? Because it is not the things of this world we are after, my friends, it is heaven we are after. The Kingdom of God.

"And I know, I know," the minister said, his thick hand raised in the air, the overhead light flashing for a moment on his spectacles. "You may ask, where am I supposed to go? Well, I'll tell you. You know we were fund-raising together for six long years. Six long years and we raised the money to build this wonderful place, our home. We picked out these chairs. This carpet. You women baked bread and cookies. You men went door-to-door. You made phone calls. We built this place together. Didn't we?"

They had.

They nodded.

"'Come out from among them and be separate,' the Lord says. There is one path to salvation, and that is the Lord Jesus Christ. And here, here in this house, this is where you will find him. Follow Him when he moves you, and I promise you. I promise you. You will be blessed. You will be so blessed."

None of the old folks from the Evening Primrose old folks' home who'd been sickened by the water ever came back to town, but those twenty-odd others who had not been sickened left, too. By mid-July the place was closed up for good. Four of Lions' six children returned from the clinic for the duration of the summer, while their parents found houses or apartments in Burnsville or Denver or Cheyenne or, in one case, back in Nebraska, and—in another case—to family in Iowa. The bank foreclosed on nineteen properties and a ranching/gas-line development company out of Greeley bought up a dozen more for cash, including the nursing home and all its structures. Over the years "For Sale" signs swung and bleached in the sun and wind until the houses were stripped and looted and eventually became safety hazards and were fenced in with chain-link.

If, once they had all gone and settled into their new apartments and condominiums in Burnsville, they were at all nostalgic, it was for a Lions that had never existed. They'd sometimes reminisce, saying the nights there had been uniformly cool and the days full of sunshine. Sugar beets and root vegetables grew as big as your head. The rooms of the schools and even the library were turned into storage rooms overflowing with grain. The name of the place, they said, came from a time when mountain lions roamed the prairie, and there's a big blond head of one of those lions—a giant male with green eyes—still mounted inside the bar that closed down years after they left. If you peer in the soaped-up windows, you can see him looking out at you.

Goodbyes didn't come singly, or one at a time, and more often than not you were lucky if you even knew you were in the midst of one. May Ransom believed—and not only for the older folks' sake—that if you had the opportunity, the ceremony of a farewell was worth it. So they said the free meal in the diner was for the Jorgensens, even though it was for everyone. Annie, Dock, and Emery came into the diner for pancakes, and to help prepare the food and decorations. Annie tied on an apron after she ate and came behind the counter to help cook. Fried chicken, country potatoes, butter beans and boiled spinach, and iced chocolate cake. Boyd was to roll a keg of Coors banquet beer over from across the street, brought in special order on the previous week's truck delivery, and anyone left in town who wanted to send off themselves or the Jorgensens, oldest of old-timers, was welcome.

May was measuring and sifting cake flour, a fine white dust floating about her chest and arms.

"I don't know how I let you talk me into living here in the first place," Boyd said.

"It wasn't talk," May looked up. "If you recall."

Annie laughed. Emery watched his mother's mouth, then moved his own in silent imitation.

"Leigh, are you going to get Georgie?"

She nodded.

Dock took a giant waxed box of produce and set it on the counter by the deep stainless steel sink. "Annie went over there yesterday and she was still in bed."

"The woman's had a loss," May said and lowered the beaters into the cake bowl. "They were married thirty-five years."

"He was gone up north or working in that shop at least fifteen of those years," Boyd said.

May shot him a look. "Don't you get everybody started."

He raised his hands. "I leave people to their own imaginations."

"Like hell you do."

May ran a stalk of celery under the faucet and shook it over the sink, the tiny beads of water lit up in the sun shining through the windows. Emery stared at it from the booth where he sat with his mother, then called out. With both hands he held up one of his green apple slices, transparent in the sunlight, and the door opened and in came Gordon with a bag of streamers and balloons, his skin scrubbed red with wind and sun, the bones in his face sharp and angular, dark circles around his eyes, and a radiance behind them. They all grew quiet. Emery jumped up and ran across the room and took Gordon's hand, and the two young men hugged. Gordon reached into his pocket and took out a kazoo.

"God help us," Boyd said.

He blew once on the kazoo and gave it to Emery, who cradled it and returned to the booth with his mother.

"Well," Gordon said, looking at Leigh. His dark hair was tangled and starting to look shaggy. He came to the counter and set down the bag. "Not much of a party atmosphere in here."

May crossed the diner, kissed Gordon's cheek, and hugged him. "We've missed you." Three honks from Emery on his kazoo.

"Where'd you get that stuff?" Leigh asked. Six honks.

"Burnsville." Two honks.

"You've been in Burnsville?" Four honks.

Annie put her hand over the kazoo. "OK, Emery," she said.

"I told your mom I'd go," Gordon said. "And I told her I'd be here."

"That's a good man, Gordon," Annie said. "Bring those balloons over here, will you? Blow one up for Emery."

In the next two hours, Gordon blew up yellow and green balloons and scrubbed the kitchen and range behind the counter, and smiled and chatted with Annie and with Boyd about the heat and the Jorgensens' emigration out of a country they'd lived in longer than anyone, after the Walkers, and he taste-tested the butter beans for May, but he did not look at Leigh again, and she thought his smiles seemed thin, and that there were lines around his eyes where there hadn't been a month before.

Leigh gave her mother a look that Gordon saw.

"I'll go get her, May," he said, and turned toward the door.

"I'll come too," Leigh said.

"You don't have to," he said.

"I'll come."

"Gordon and Leigh," May called out across the diner without looking up from the silverware she was rolling in paper napkins. "Go get Georgie."

They climbed in the truck and from the diner to the front-age road did not speak.

"So you've been in Burnsville this whole time? A week?"

"No," he said.

"Where then?"

"Up north."

"Where do you stay?"

"I camp."

"There's no little house up there?"

"Actually," he said, watching the road, "there sort of is."

"People are mad at you for going."

He slowed and looked sideways at her. "Are they?"

"Pretty mad."

"I'm sorry to hear that."

"You missed my birthday."

Gordon was quiet.

"Maybe you should quit going up there," Leigh said.

"Maybe I should."

"Unless it's really important. Unless you're like"—she made a strange gesture with her hands—"going to visit Boggs or something."

He watched her hands settle in her lap.

"You're not," she said. "Are you?"

"Leigh," he said.

"Why do you keep going?"

"If I told you I went up there just to be alone, would you believe me?"

"Why would you do that?"

He glanced at her.

"Well?"

He was quiet a few moments. "Would you believe me?"

"If you wanted me to."

"OK, then. I go up there just to be alone."

"Where your dad used to go?"

He kept his eyes on the road. "Yes."

"Tell me about it."

So he told her about it. How it seemed despite the speed and wheels turning against the pavement as he drove, there was no movement at all. How big it all was. Insofar as Lions was a place of air and light and rock, he was not so much driving out of town as he was driving deeper into it, beneath it, say, or within it. It felt like a dropping down, not a driving away.

"It's so quiet," he told her, "so empty. Everything you thought was important disappears." He held his fingertips lightly together, then burst them open, fingers spread wide. "Just like that."

She looked at him skeptically. "Everything like what disappears?"

"All the plans. Making something of yourself."

She looked out the window.

"Is that so crazy?" he asked.

She shrugged. She got that feeling of emptiness in the middle of Lions, every day, and you could have called it despair, or panic, or desperation to get out, but you couldn't call it a good or wholesome thing. And you didn't need to drive up north to find it.

"I didn't mean to hurt your feelings, Leigh."

She kept her gaze pointed out the window. "You didn't hurt my feelings."

"Tell me what's been happening around here." He squeezed her hand, and the contact between them dissolved some of the tension. She moved closer to him in the front seat, yet not quite to where she'd used to sit, in the middle.

"You know about that man in the water tower?"

Gordon nodded.

"I saw him. I went with Boyd and he followed Chuck and the firetruck."

"They shouldn't have let you."

"I didn't want to mention it at the funeral. But I can't get his face out of my head."

"I'm sorry." He reached across her shoulder and pulled her in close. Kissed the crown of her head.

She counted off the names of everyone she could remember who'd left, or was planning to leave. "And none of them even saw him."

"Does my mom know about everyone going?"

"It's sort of hard to tell," she said, and he nodded. "Do you think she'll stay?"

"Yes."

That night she dreamt of a lion.

It was late in the day, and warm. Around her feet, little yellow cup-shaped flowers. Gordon just before her. The red factory bricks behind them flushed with rosy light, and the windows of their houses and John Walker's truck in the driveway in the distance blinking with reflected gold.

She was digging for treasure while Gordon studied the horizon. Suddenly his face flattened. His gaze was fixed behind her and she turned slowly, filled with dread, until she saw it, too: a massive lion, fifty yards off, in the grass and weeds. Full mane. Each paw the size of her head. Eyes of fire. She could smell its gamey breath. The blood in her veins went hot and she froze.

It took her breath away. She couldn't call out and she couldn't move. The lion's eyes looked at her the way all the eyes of all the birds and stray dogs and cats and wild creatures she'd ever seen had looked at her, as if with the same pair of eyes.

I didn't think there were really lions here, she somehow finally communicated without speaking, and dropped her spade.

Then she understood that it hadn't come for her. Perhaps it hadn't even come at all. Perhaps it had been here all that time, for Gordon.

"It's true," Gordon said, as his face was slowly erased. "It follows me everywhere now."

July Fourth weekend someone put a sign up on the highway at the westbound Lions exit that said *living ghost town* stenciled in white paint on a piece of black painted plywood. There was a longer line than usual of college students and families and truckers all heading west pulled off the highway and stopped at May's for sandwiches, french fries, ice cream sundaes. Easily twice the regular business the Lucy Graves had seen in years. Every one of the customers, it seemed, had come into town looking for an imaginary city. A haunted hotel. Cowboys and horses. A gold mine. A saloon.

May rolled her eyes at it but was pleased by the traffic. Boyd had to go twice to Burnsville to get more sandwich bread, cold cuts, ground beef, and instant spuds. They came in off the highway from Omaha, Lincoln, Cheyenne, Kansas City, Cedar Rapids, Des Moines. The diner was a lark. A live museum. What was this place, they wondered, stepping out of their cars on the deserted, preternaturally quiet main street in town. Marybeth Sharpe waved at them all from her rocking chair. They rooted around in her musty, shadowy store and bought crystal doorknobs and rusting metal plate advertisements for Angel soap and John Deere tractors and they bought tarnished hunting knives in sheaths of needlepointed roses and rotted leather, and spoons

of solid silver. After they left, Marybeth walked crookedly into
the diner, grinning wide, and laid a dollar bill down in front of
each customer, as a gift.

A journalist from Greeley came in early one day. Outside,
the hot, white sky hung low. The diner was crowded, and the journalist took a seat at the lunch counter. She had smart, smooth,
dark hair, wore sandals with hiking soles, and kept a slim, silver
computer in a satchel over one shoulder.

When Leigh greeted her, the woman asked if she knew anything about the man who'd come into town and been drowned
in the water tower.

"Nobody drowned him," Leigh said. "He drowned himself."

"Are you sure?"

Leigh shrugged.

"Did any of you have contact with him?"

"Coffee?" Leigh asked.

"Sure."

Leigh poured the woman a cup and handed her a laminated
menu. "Where are you from?"

"Greeley."

"You're writing a story?"

"Don't you think it's curious? The man drowned in the
water supply? It used to happen in the early 1900s. But there's
been no record of such a death in this state for almost a century.
What do you make of that?"

Leigh shrugged. "What do you?"

"It happened in Lions in 1923. Did you know that?"

"No."

"It was a single man. A wanderer."

"Really." Leigh considered. "In a long coat?"

"A duster."

"What's that?"

"Old-fashioned version of a long coat."

"Did he have a dog?"

"A dog?"

"This guy had a dog. Did anyone tell you about the dog?" As Leigh told the story, the woman drew her hand to her mouth and shook her head.

"Can you show me?"

"There's a white cross on the highway."

The woman made a note.

"Did you hear about the broken window over there?" Leigh asked.

"He was here in town?"

"No one told you about what happened in the bar?"

Annie Sterling spent an afternoon with Emery and Gordon in Marybeth's shop looking through old, flaking, yellow newspapers that came apart in her hands, but found nothing that went as far back as 1923, and they could find no evidence of any other water tower drowning. Emery found an old curry comb he ran back and forth over the short grass. Gordon found a foot-long cast-iron mermaid on a stand that, if planted outside, would appear as though she were drifting at sea atop of a swath of high grass, hands interlaced behind her head. The ends of her fins were thin and ragged with rust, but the elliptical metal scales of her fish tail were immaculately, symmetrically fused. It looked to Gordon like each one had been individually molded. He shook his head in wonder and appreciation at what one of his grandfathers had no doubt made. The mermaid's lips were parted, and her breasts pointed through the loose ends of her hair.

"Modeled after one of your grandmothers," Georgianna said, surveying the mermaid's face, then touching the bridge of its nose. "Anna. Or Ruth."

"I think it's older than that, Mom."

"Louise, then. Or Sarah."

Gordon set her in the front yard, suspended among eight-inch-high foxtails as if she were floating on her back among them. Totally unaware, everyone said, of a mermaid's link to floods, storms, shipwrecks, and drownings, to spirits who would trap a man in a place he ought to know to flee.

Boy doesn't even realize he's drowning, they said.

Somebody ought to tell him.

Dock called the Greeley journalist who said she'd found the story of the drowned wanderer in a collection of bound public planning documents in a local library. She said she'd send copies along but never did.

"Too busy," Dock said.

"It's because there's no such document," May said.

"This is the newspaper," Dock said. "She can't just make shit up."

Somehow, the echo of this narrow, dark-clothed man coming to town and drowning in the tower felt real to them. So many of them had seen the man who'd recently drowned. You could dismiss stories like these when they hadn't touched you. This one had touched them.

They tried to imagine it, so many decades ago, same heat, same dust, same spirit of flight out of town, same longing and despair, and a tall, thin man in a dark coat coming to usher in the rest of the bad news. It gave one the sense of a long timeline of history folding up like a neat accordion of typewritten paper into a single carefully layered moment. It gave one the sense of a mirror hung somehow, somewhere in the empty space of Jefferson Street—the way heat could double and distort the inventory of the town, make the air in the distance shine and buckle and reflect little houses hung upside down in the vacant blue.

After her shift one afternoon at the end of July, Leigh found Gordon in the shop. She stood in a doorway of glaring light. He was standing beside the workbench, his fingertips on an old iron vice. He looked up.

"Why're you just standing there?" She crossed the shop and picked up his fingers. He had no lights, fans, or machines running. She wrapped his arms around her own waist and interlaced her fingers behind his neck. For a moment she rested her cheek against his chest, but when she looked up at him, his eyes were streaming tears. He smiled and drew his sleeve across his face. Nothing but the wind and light pouring in through the open door and the chinks in the piled metal and sifting through their loose hair. There was color in his cheeks, and his dark curls were an overgrown mess. He was there and not, Gordon, and not. She backed up to the workbench and sat on it.

"You look like your dad."

"Do I?"

"Have you eaten at all in the past week?"

"I miss him."

She took his hand. "Let me ask you a question, though, Gordon. OK?"

"Go ahead."

"I don't mean any offense by it at all."

"OK."

"Do you think he was happy?"

"My dad?"

"Yes, your dad. Do you think he was happy?"

They were both picturing John Walker, then. Skinny, bespectacled, standing outside of the shop, wind blowing white wisps of his hair. Aloof. His gaze pointed at something no one else could see. Light as the air around him.

"I've been thinking about that a lot," Gordon said. He was quiet a minute. Two. He took his hand from Leigh's and sat up on the workbench alongside her and put his hand back on the old, red Wilton table vice. "I've been thinking that any wish, anything at all that a person might wish for," he paused—his father had not been a man of wishes—"is like a branch being offered to a drowning man." Show him anyone who lives for their home, he thought, for their family, or job, or for anything at all, and he'd show you a miserable person. A person who would hang on to that thing no matter how awful it was.

"That's what I mean," Leigh said. "A person needs a branch."

Gordon blinked and wrapped his fingers around the cast steel of the vice.

She scooted closer to him, and reached her arm around his back and set her hand on his fingers. The metal vice was cool and solid. "I know what you're thinking. I know you think you have to stay here. That you're bound to this place. I understand more than you realize. Even if you're not telling me everything."

"You do?"

She nodded, and he moved his fingers over the top of her hand. "And Gordon. I think you should leave it behind."

"Leave what behind?"

"All of it. Come with me to school. Like we planned. Like you promised. It's the next thing to do."

"The next thing to do."

"Why when you say that does it sound like a stupid idea? Gordon. Come on. We can't stay here. You can't stay here."

He just looked at her.

"I can't go alone," she said.

"Sure you could."

It was as if he'd slapped her. "You would just send me off?" She pulled her hand back.

"I wouldn't be sending you off."

"Think about it," she said. "You could turn over the shop to Dock long term. Think of what it'd mean to him and Emery."

He was quiet a moment. "That's true."

"Say you will?"

"Ah, Leigh."

"It's supposed to be us," she said. "Together out there."

"I know it."

"Come with me. We'll make a clean break. We'll start over."

"I don't need to start over."

"Yes," she said, "you do."

He shook his head. "What about my mom? All my dad's work. His life's work, Leigh."

She blinked. "Welding?"

He studied her. Welding, she'd said.

Sometime the winter before—a Sunday afternoon—he remembered exactly the moment in the shop, he was practicing with the plasma cutter on the thin aluminum of some of Jorgensen's irrigation pipe that'd been damaged in the last season, and suddenly without any effort on his part he sensed something else about the work. He wasn't welding; the welding was happening.

He was high on the experience for a week.

"Get your head out of the clouds," his father finally said, handing him a set of pliers, but there was a light in his eye as he said it. The pliers were cold and heavy in Gordon's hand. The rubber sleeves over its handles were a bright kingfisher blue. "Going to hurt yourself," his father said, turning away. "Or both of us."

So then it was just welding again. You marked up the plan. You cleaned the metal. You set your voltage and feed speed and did the job.

Still. He'd seen that look in his father's eye. It was a look that said yes, and there's more where that came from.

"Don't you want something better?" Leigh asked.

He shrugged.

"Think of Emery and Dock. Think of Annie. Living people. Who could use the work while you're away. If there even is any. Would you hoard it for yourself? That doesn't sound like you. Or your dad."

"I guess that's true."

"Have you seen Dock's alfalfa? Isn't it strange not to see Jorgensen's wheat ripening? Doesn't any of this strike you as significant? Signs, Gordon."

"Signs," he said, without interest.

"It's the responsible thing to do."

"I don't know."

"Tell me you'll try it for a month. One month."

"What if instead I asked you to stay here?"

"I'd say you didn't know what you were asking." She crossed her arms. Just stay there? Like what, a year? Five? Ten? Doing what? Waiting for him?

There's one about that kind of mistake, too. Today, where the old highway connects with the frontage road that takes you to the new highway, there's a one-room schoolhouse that appears and disappears among the giant papery green docks and goosefoot-shaped leaves of lambsquarter. When it's lit up, you can see the old brass bell tolling, though it makes no sound. When Leigh was a girl, she begged May to tell and retell the tale.

A woman from out east who had once been the school-teacher, a twenty-six-year-old Honora Strong, was held responsible for the death of every single one of her nineteen young students, aged four to fifteen, frozen to death in a sudden, late-spring blizzard. Though she herself didn't survive to be hanged or cast out for it, she was caught forever on the highway looking for them. Sometimes in a high wind, you can hear them crying, and her calling them by name.

She lived in a room adjacent to the schoolhouse, with a bedstead and a stove, and had sent her students home, hoping they'd be ahead of the storm, because she was expecting a lover. He went by Miller—David Wayne Miller—and he had been see-ing her off and on for two years as he traversed the countryside, east to west and north to south. He was from Utah, though his family were Germans and Swedes out of South Dakota. He had small eyes the color of stone, dark hair raked with silver, and a barrel-shaped torso. Though he wasn't a tall man, he called himself a big guy, which was accurate in the sense that he took up all the space in a room, left none for anyone else to talk, nor air for them to breathe. He had, somewhere, a wife and two children—and had, somewhere else, another wife, and another child. To all of his women he made promises he couldn't keep, and left each one of them trapped in her hometown, waiting for him to make good.

Like so many of the westerners who broke the land and occupied positions of influence, May told Leigh—the sheets and yellow wool blanket pulled up to her chin, her small white fingers curled around the satin binding—David Wayne Miller was a sunny liar, a good storyteller, a hard worker, and an expert, cold-hearted son of a bitch. He came out of every shoot-out, every rotten horse trade, and every madam's house smelling like a rose. For every crime he committed, for every life he ruined, there was a fabulous story to stand in for the truth.

"And you know what?" May asked her daughter. "People loved the stories. They wanted them. People say they want the truth but they don't. They want a story."

"I want a story."

"I know you do."

According to the historical record, David Wayne Miller was seen some five or six years after the death of Honora Strong and her students, in Deadwood, in a gunfight with a man who was no better than he was and who thus recognized a sick man when he saw one. Miller survived the fight, and, it is said, took up a stethoscope and paraded around the West as a traveling surgeon praised for his healing arts, and died rich, fat, and happy at an old age on a ranch in southeast Wyoming.

"Green River?" Leigh asked her mother from her narrow bed.

"Couldn't say."

"Rawlins?"

"Not telling."

"But he's dead? For sure?"

"There is no man more dead than this man."

Nobody could guess where the schoolteacher had met him. Once Honora could see Miller wasn't coming that frigid spring day, and the windows were half blocked with blue snow, then within an hour completely blocked and blackened, and there was no more wood in the box to burn, and it was hours before dawn, she confessed the entire matter in writing. In the days after, children were exhumed out of their empire of snow, their pointed faces blue, their eyelashes frosted with ice. The schoolteacher was likewise discovered, the confession stuffed in her frozen bosom.

A world of hurt. That, May Ransom told her daughter, is what comes of choosing the wrong man in the wrong place at the wrong time. And then waiting for him, waiting for him. There are good and decent men in this world, she told her daughter, and there are men like he was: touched by darkness and, eventually, overcome by it.

When the old schoolhouse materializes out of nothing on the side of the road, it's as clean and white as the day it was built, the bright bell shining in its square-shaped wooden tower, and passersby from behind the windshields of their Pontiacs and Hondas, driving from Chicago to LA or Omaha to Reno, have seen the poor woman right beside it in a long brown- and rose-colored dress, her thick, curling red hair blowing as if she, alone, were on fire in the midst of a terrible storm.

Such tales of children and their schoolteachers or bus drivers caught in sudden snowstorms on the plain are all too common; some still say that David Wayne Miller is behind the death of every one of them.

"Because every wrong man," May told Leigh every time, while the girl watched the shadows of the cottonwood bend and lengthen on the wall behind her mother's head, "is the same wrong man."

First day of August. A light, circling wind blew the heat around the county like fever breath, lifting the dust from the fallow fields and wheeling around and dropping it again in a thin brown cloud over the surface of the town. Over the last couple weeks on her way to and from the diner Leigh watched the yarrow and Queen Anne's lace cracking, splitting, and breaking into a powder that fell apart and slowly resolved itself into the pale dirt. "A coalescence," John Walker had once told her, drawing his finger along the seam of a weld on the chicken coop.

In every direction mirages of false rivers and lakes, the scant trees hovering upside down in the buckled glare. If the world were any one thing it was light—refracted, diffused, reflected, and smashed and split apart by metal roofing and run-down cars, their once bright green and yellow and red paint now muted and spotted with rust, their windows broken, their plaintive faces lopsided on a cracked chassis or missing wheels. It was so much light you could scarcely see, and Leigh's eyes were squinted all the time, and her head ached, and she longed for night. She imagined a house by the ocean. A house on a river. A house on a lake. Cool rooms and shady gardens and a green twilight. She imagined rainy nights. Tiered water fountains elaborate as wedding cakes.

When Gordon was home he was in the shop dressed in wool and sweating, repairing a broken johnny bar, cleaning the tools and machines, standing in the open shop door holding cold black coffee in the ceramic blue mug he'd always used, speckled like an egg, John's solid brown mug still in its place beside the old radio.

When he was in the house he was heating up canned spaghetti or baked beans for himself and Georgianna, urging her to dress, sweeping the floors and washing sheets and towels. Or he was sitting in his father's chair, rereading his old paperbacks, small and familiar in his hands, dried glue cracking at their seams, yellowed pages soft as felt.

Twice Leigh brought sandwiches from the Lucy Graves and they walked across the bony ground to the factory where they ate quietly, side by side, not touching, commenting on the heat, or the swallows nesting in mud huts along the rafters. The floor was dirty, the bricks were broken. Leigh couldn't remember what had ever seemed magical in the old ruin. Most times she asked him, Gordon didn't want to go.

One morning, Gordon in the shop and Leigh at the diner, the man from Denver whose family owned a string of tire and oil change shops across the state finally came out to make, he said, some kind of assessment of the garage, the town's only open business other than the Gas & Grocer, diner, bar, and Marybeth's. His name was Alan Ranger and his eyes were blue as enamel, his hair bright as dry ricks of hay, and he wore a blond Fu Manchu Leigh could not look at without imagining kissing his face. It surprised her, and made her own face hot.

"What are you doing in this town?" he asked when Leigh set down his club sandwich and french fries.

"Packing."

"Good answer." He looked at the sandwich doubtfully. "What are those?"

"Decorative toothpicks."

"I didn't order those."

"Would you like me to remove them?"

"Please."

"You want anything other than water?"

"You serve beer?"

"Across the street. Boyd'll serve 'em to go."

"Now that," he said, "is what I call useful information."

"She's got a boyfriend," May said, coming up behind Leigh with a tray propped on her hand.

"I do not."

"Girl says she don't," Alan Ranger said, and popped a french fry into his mouth.

"Well," May said, "she *do.*" She crossed the diner and set down three slices of pie and ice cream at a far table. He locked eyes with Leigh. "Whoever Mr. Nobody is he ought to know better than to leave her out alone among the wolves."

May circled back to the range. "That," she said, "I'll give you. Leigh. Take this order over to Georgie."

Leigh opened the box and peered in at the sliced ham with hot cherry jam and green beans. "She's got a ton of food."

"Take it or you're fired."

When Leigh left Georgianna's kitchen, there he was, parked in front of the Walkers' house. He drove a forest green pickup, his golden arm hanging out the window. He smiled, and she leaned in at the rolled-down window. There was a six-pack of cold brown bottles in the passenger seat.

"Your mama doesn't like the competition," he said. "Bet she used to be the prettiest one here."

"Please."

He nodded at the six-pack. "Know a good place to go have a cold beer?"

They walked out across the empty fields behind the Walker and Ransom houses to the factory. In the distance, west of the road, the ragged field, hard as tack and scabbed with weeds. Leigh crawled beneath the chain-link and Alan Ranger followed. She laughed at him.

"Why you laughing at me?"

"You look funny," she said, "grown man shimmying under a fence."

"Well," he brushed off the legs of his jeans. "I came in pursuit of a very particular thing."

They sat in the sun with the warm bricks against their backs. He opened two of the bottles and raised his. Leigh raised her own.

"Born and raised?" he asked, scanning the horizon.

"Yep."

"Ever been out?"

"Nope."

"Your guy never took you out?"

"Not out of here."

"What are you waiting on? Hell, girl. You won't be this pretty forever. Want me to take you back to Denver with me?"

"Come on."

"It's cooler there."

"Liar."

"No, no" he said. "Nice restaurants. Nice neighborhoods. Nice little house, right? Big kitchen. Big bedroom. Buy you pretty dresses, take you to church on Sundays. Make a couple babies."

She rolled her eyes but smiled.

"I'll give you my number. You have a car?"

"I might have one I can use."

"Come out to Denver."

"I'd come out to Denver."

"I'll show you around, girl."

"Yeah?"

"Hell, yeah. Ought to share yourself with the world. Instead of hiding away with this boyfriend you say you don't have."

She drank two beers and he drank four. They lined up the empties and tossed pebbles toward their round mouths. A stray brown and white barn cat with a milky white ghost eye watched Alan from a distance. She could see the sun glinting on the metal of the Quonset hut, and knew Gordon was in there welding. He had his head down working. It was what he did.

"He's a fool," Alan told her.

"Prettiest girl I've seen across this whole state," he told her.

"You should move to California. That's where a girl like you belongs," he told her. "Long white dress on the beach. Hair piled up on your head like this?" He reached over and put his hands in her hair. She felt her heart beating.

"You must be dying here," he said.

"He's got you trapped here, doesn't he?"

"Tell you what, whoever he is, he don't deserve you."

"If he knew what you were worth, he wouldn't leave you alone at an empty building with a guy like me."

"He ever kiss you?" he asked, and leaned toward her. She raised her hand as if to push him away, then rested her fingertips on his T-shirt. "Like that?"

The kissing went on for some time. She felt drunk. Blindly happy. She bunched his T-shirt in her hand, right there at his chest where she'd set her fingers. He made a laughing sound in his open mouth when she did that. Then he moved his own hand to beneath the hem of her T-shirt, and she pulled back.

"Oh, come on," he said, leaning back in, pressing the shape of a smile against her mouth.

She pulled back again, then stood up.

"Oh, hell," he said, getting to his feet. "You don't play coy very good." He took the last empty by the neck and swung it flashing in the daylight out into the dirt. "Been inside?"

"All the time."

"Show me."

She hesitated.

He took her arm and led her through the open doorway, into the shadow.

"I can't."

He stopped and looked back at her. "Are you serious?" His smile faded.

"Sorry," she said. He dropped her arm.

"Sweetheart. You've been playing along all afternoon. Look at me and tell me you don't want to stay in here with me a little while."

She stared at the dirt.

"Tell you what," he said. "My garage is the only viable business in this town for a hundred-mile radius. Any man here who isn't sweeping you up under his arm and hauling you out to someplace just as pretty as you are, he's a jackass, plain and simple."

It embarrassed her for Gordon.

"Tell me you didn't like that just now," he said. "Tell me you weren't thinking about it all morning."

She said nothing.

"You owe me for two beers," he said. He put out his hand. She gave him four dollars and he turned and stepped into the daylight.

She walked to the diner for the dinner shift. May was in the doorway looking out at the street. She stepped aside to let her daughter inside. "You stupid, stupid girl."

Leigh took her apron from the peg on the back of the door and tied it behind her neck and around her waist. May came in and stood right behind Leigh and talked to her back.

"Gordon was here."

Leigh said nothing.

"I asked him if he wanted sandwiches, if you were going to the factory later tonight. He wouldn't even look at me Leigh."

Leigh's heart started racing. "What does that have to do with me?"

"Please."

The paint was cracked and chipping away at the dusty chair rail that ran behind the ice bin. Leigh crossed her arms. "You know what? There are some things Gordon just can't and won't ever do."

"You've got that right."

She could hear her mother pulling produce out of the cooler.

"If there's one thing you should've learned from John Walker," May said, "it's that you make big decisions the way you make small decisions. And I hope to god you didn't just do what I think you did."

"I'm not stupid," Leigh said, her face hot. She turned around.

"No," May said, handing Leigh the handwritten specials to put on the chalkboard. "You're about half stupid. You ought to at least be smart enough to know that you're not as pretty as men will say you are."

"Oh, thanks a lot."

"God, Leigh. It's not personal."

"I don't want to live here forever you know." She climbed up on the stool with the chalk and list in her fist.

"No one is saying you should."

Leigh stared at the words of the lunch special without reading them.

"I wish you'd use the stepladder," May said.

"I'm fine."

"Erase that real good," May said.

"I know."

"Denver's the same as here. Only bigger. You'd find a restaurant just like ours, twice as big with ten times as many customers and all the same grief."

"I'm not going to college to wait tables."

"Oh I see. College is going to open all the doors. Is that what?"

"Maybe I'll go to California."

"Now there's an original idea."

"Why are you so mean to me?"

"I'm not."

"What am I supposed to do?"

"Scrub and peel and slice these carrots. Both bags."

She was to meet Gordon outside the shop at seven-thirty that night, and waited until the light reflected on the empty water tower went from white to gold to rose to black, but he never came. He'd be checking into the North Star by now. She could picture it.

The road he'd follow north from the motel would slowly break up and give way to higher, empty, treeless desert pocked with stones, where he'd come to the house. It'd be peculiarly narrow and high, fashioned of rough-hewn logs with a sharp, pointed metal roof. The beads on the roof would be John's, or his father's, or grandfather's: perfect, straight, clean. In a rough circle around the place, fine gravel, glacial till, fossilized bones of fishes. The windows of the place would always be dark. According to his father's directions, he was to take the canned food and the wool blanket and books from the trunk, and bring it all to the door, and knock on it. Simple.

On every visit, he'd take the grocery bags and hurry them to the front door to get out of the wind. It would always give him the chills; it would always feel like upon knocking at that door, his life was changing. How must it have been that first time? That was the day he stepped out of her reach, forever. He'd knock, and get no response. It would be a steel-backed white door, the kind John admired for its simplicity and versatility. The kind he had put on the back of the shop two years previous, and Gordon would know instinctively that his father had bought two at once, and drove the other up north in the truck and installed

it. Inside, behind that door in the little house, there'd be a red
painted iron kettle on a pedestal-mounted woodstove that John
would have fashioned himself. There'd be little blue checked
curtains, stitched by Georgianna, over a single window. Firewood
stacked neatly outside a little back door that John had bucked
and split himself.

Gordon would knock again, listening. Nothing. He could
have left, then. He'd driven up as he said he would. For months
afterward, he must have returned to this moment. He might have
turned away with no idea of what service he was refusing, and
so never have been troubled by his conscience—only, perhaps,
by nagging curiosity. He might have stepped casually from that
doorstep through the wind to his father's truck. There could
have been cold beer and road trips, college, girls, rivers and
mountains, books, art, music, little successes . . . all the things
he'd see as if from a great distance in the months to come. There
could have been all of those things.

You can say no, his father had told him.

Gordon would knock once more that first visit, and put his
ear to the door. He'd touch the doorknob. Cold metal. He'd turn
it, and the door would open.

"John? Is that you?" From deep inside the room on the
other side of the door, the voice of a young man.

You wanted magic in the world, Leigh thought, but not like
that. People didn't live for a hundred and twenty years. Hundred
and fifty. Or if they did, it wasn't alone in the wide-open country,
with no one to help them. Or if they were out there, they weren't
people that young men like Gordon were supposed to tie their
lives to.

But of course none of the Walkers would have called their lives, or this task, hard; she could imagine what John Walker would say of it, if she were able to ask him. He'd say that it'd never been a sacrifice, that it hadn't trapped him in Lions, that he'd never even made a decision about it, that's what real freedom was.

No choice in the matter, he'd say from his chair, looking up at her over the edge of a paperback in the orange lamplight. There's nowhere else to go, anyway, Miss Ransom. Then he'd gesture around the old living room. Isn't this paradise enough for you?

But these Walkers were a different breed.

Lions was no paradise, and she had taken no vow.

Before he left, Jorgensen sold his water rights outright and put the house up, though it would never sell. By the end of the summer, the once-creamy white porch where he and Dorrie raised their five children would be burnt with a broad shadow of brown dust and spray painted with glyphs and giant black letters so that if you saw it from a distance the old farmstead resembled a farmhouse no more than a ruined boxcar.

When Leigh saw it, she imagined slim young men and women in blue jeans and dark T-shirts sliding off the highway in neutral and sneaking out of their cars to circle every empty lot and print the beautiful old houses with code. She stood before the graffiti trying to decipher it, black grasshoppers knocking softly against her ankles. The unfamiliar characters could have been symbols for anything, but their jaggedness and backwardness—all the figures like people with their backs turned or with hands up in postures of defense—seemed to her messages of warning.

By this second week of August the West Wind motel was cleared out of beds and desks and sheets and towels, and Gordon had been gone another four days. Five.

Alan Ranger fired Levon, the manager at the garage, as well as his two employees, and brought them into the bar for beers and shots, afterward, where he offered them jobs in Denver. They took him at his word and left with their Burnsville girlfriends by week's end. On her way to the diner later that weekend, Leigh stopped outside the old garage and looked up above the store at the window with the blue checked curtain where Levon Carrothers and his father, Alison, had lived as long as she could remember. For a while when she was a girl they even called it Carrothers' Garage, then it got bought up, which was a help to them. There was a peeling, cracked yellow sticker on the window that read: Good Work Done Good. Inside, the garage was empty. The office was locked, but the sign was still turned to OPEN.

"The garage is really closed," Leigh said when she walked into the diner for the breakfast shift.

"And took three men with it," Boyd said, spooning sugar into his coffee. "Some nerve that guy had, being all chummy like that, right after he fires them."

"He's just doing his job," May said, turning his eggs. She looked at Leigh. "Least he spent a little money in town. That was considerate."

"More attentive than some people," Leigh said.

"Really, Leigh. Maybe Gordon didn't want to be around to see his father die. And to watch his mother lose her marbles. Or watch his girl take off with out-of-town management or some big dope from Burnsville."

Boyd raised his eyebrows and looked at Leigh. "Jesus, girl. It wouldn't kill you to spend a little time alone."

She stepped behind the register and stooped as if she were looking for something in the shelves below and put her hands to her temples and shut her eyes.

"That guy was married, too," Boyd said. "Just so you know. Or didn't you mind?"

Leigh stood up and brushed off her shirt. "You have a lot of nerve. If I were you I'd talk a lot less."

"What's that supposed to mean?"

"It means everything happening around here is your fault and everybody knows it."

"Alright," May said. "Enough."

"Hope your stupid joke was worth it."

"Enough, Leigh. Go."

"Dock told me the joke from that night. It wasn't even funny."

"I hadn't finished telling it!" Boyd's eyes widened. "Wait. Dock was talking about this?"

"Enough!" May yelled.

"He told all of us," Leigh said.

"All of who? When?"

May put her hands on Leigh's shoulders and turned her toward the door. "Out."

"I thought I was working."

"Out."

"I need the money."

"Go."

"Was Dock talking about me?" she heard Boyd say as she stepped out over the sidewalk, his voice high and thin.

Leigh stepped into the empty street. Only eight o'clock and already her forehead and temple ached from squinting in the blazing light. It'd started in the bathroom, slicing into the mirror from the window as she brushed her teeth. The heat had beaten the earth and the pavement and the rooftops of empty houses to a metallic sheen and reduced the horizon to the same thin white iridescence in every direction. Thirteen days, she said under her breath, over and over, with every step back home.

Poor girl, those remaining in town said, even as they packed. Darkness of this place is sucking her in.

What a waste that'd be, they said.

She was always a good girl.

Smart girl.

Pretty girl.

Go get the world, they told her whenever they could—in the diner, on the street. It wants you.

She knew it did. She heard it calling. Everyday the world came into the Lucy Graves and announced itself, then slipped back out the glass door and down the highway, out of her reach. All her life, she had measured the goodness of the world by her happiness with it. Now it was teasing her. Toward everyone her age who came into the diner she felt a nauseating combination of admiration, fear, and resentment. She was bothered that others had what looked to her like a better life. Their easy smiles, their confidence. She hated everything she envied, and she envied everyone.

She thought to pierce her nose, one of those tiny silver studs. She'd lighten her hair. She'd get a tattoo, something feminine. A bracelet around her ankle. She'd become an environmentalist. Maybe she'd become a vegetarian. Each new idea presented itself as she poured coffee, refilled water, distributed ketchup and ranch dressing.

It was as though she and Gordon had been childhood friends on the top of a dizzying precipice, and now he was falling down one side of it, and she the other. At the top there'd been summer rain and moonlight, and the thrill of exploring each other's bodies and making plans. There had been intoxicating, aerial views of the world, all of it laid out for them to enjoy. Now her own view was so foreshortened, the strangers around her brought up so close, she could neither see past them nor make out their faces.

Years from now, she'd remember with a nameless unease the way the hot days of that June, July, then August unspooled as she dished out pie and ice cream and fried sandwiches and coffee and Cokes to travelers speeding down the interstate on their adventures and stopping in the diner where she, a ghost in a ghost town, was stuck in place to serve them. She'd remember the whole town in a state of decay as Jorgensen moved away, Gordon still collecting junk from Marybeth and setting it out in the yard beneath the sun with the strange faith of a man scattering seeds across the hard ground. A film of dust settling over the old, red-painted stoop before the closed hardware store.

Years from now, she'd sit alone behind the sugar beet factory as a single magpie dove from right to left in a sharp and angry V above her head, realizing she'd spent her entire life either excited or depressed. Seeing that the last days of her last true summer were ravished by craving. She'd try to imagine a series of events, or gifts, or situations that would have satisfied her at seventeen and eighteen, and then later at twenty-five, thirty. Truth is, nothing would have. Not recognition from all the world that the family she might raise would be bright and worthwhile, not a house in the hills, not the prairie with all the wild grass still in her, not the cold moon itself in her hands or all the metal-pointed stars at her command.

Gordon returned from the north country at midnight days before they were to leave for school, and woke the following morning in his room to the sound of Leigh's voice. A distant buzz, the sheets over his bare legs. He understood she was speaking from far away. Downstairs. In the kitchen with Georgianna. Their white faces floating in the early morning light as they talked over toast and coffee. Their voices pulsed like a radio signal moving in and out of static.

". . . like his father . . ."

"I know."

". . . to be alone."

"But supposing . . ."

". . . a little patience."

"But supposing."

A silence. The ringing of spoons against coffee cups.

". . . John's father, too . . ."

". . . like a ceremony . . ."

". . . like sleep . . ."

"More toast?"

A silence, the scrape of wooden chair legs across the floor, and he went back under, the women's voices leading him on a filament of words like a path that loses itself in the dark.

In his dream his father handed him a dull and dented old copper cup—the kind you'd find in the junk shop—and told him to drink. Gordon took it for whiskey, and perhaps it was.

"What is it?" his father asked when Gordon had tasted it.

"Bitter," he said, and let the taste of it stain his tongue and the back of his throat. "And good."

When he woke again, his mother was beside him. Shadows circled her eyes like holes burned through white paper.

"You slept all day again," she said.

"I did?"

"Leigh was here."

"I know."

"I have a can of soup heated on the stove," she said. "Tomato rice. You need to eat."

He sat up. "Did you have any?"

She put her hand to her stomach and shook her head.

"Sick?"

"And a headache."

"You look skinny."

"So do you."

"You need to eat."

She drew her lips into her mouth and nodded. "It's hard to be here in the house, isn't it?"

He nodded. "Shop, too."

"He worked so hard, Gordon."

"I know."

"Too hard."

"Maybe," he said.

"No one appreciated it."

"Sure they did, Ma."

"Do you think so?"

"Yes."

"People say things about him."

"No they don't."

"They say he wasn't good to us."

"You know that isn't true."

"They say he should have moved us somewhere better."

"Did Leigh tell you that?"

"She wants the world, Gordon."

"I know it," he said. "It wants her back."

"Have you asked her to stay?"

"I don't think she can."

"I always thought she'd be able to."

He rose and left the room. He brought up two mugs of the warm, reddish-orange soup, and two slices of buttered sandwich bread. Two old metal spoons. He carried it up on the tray his father had used for Georgianna on Mother's Day and her birthday, a golden brown wicker tray with woven handles of dried willow.

They sat in the quiet and ate their bread. The moonlight cast a slant, pale blue window frame across the scratched wooden floor. It was past midnight. No birds. No sound at all. Georgianna sat with her hands around the mug in her lap. Her hair seemed no longer steel and iron but silver and white. She used to clip up the sides, but now it hung all around her. It was so long. He'd never realized it was so long.

"I can't sleep in that bed, Gordon."

"It's OK."

"I've been sleeping here," she said. "In yours."

"I know." He took her hand and pulled her from the chair and she curled up beside him. "It's OK."

"Sometimes I think I'm having a heart attack, too," she whispered.

He shut his eyes and held his breath high up in his chest. "Me, too."

When he was sure she'd fallen asleep, Gordon stood and crossed the yard to the shop where he stretched out on the floor, lengthwise beside the workbench.

Dock and Emery were there just after dawn, ready to work and knocking on the door. Gordon rose stiffly, rubbed his eyes, and opened the side door. He reached out to shake Dock's hand, and Dock pulled him in for a hug.

"Where you been boy?"

Gordon smiled and hugged back. Emery stepped up for his turn, nearly crushing Gordon's rib cage with his wiry arms.

"Sorry to barge in on you," Dock said. "Emery's been chomping at the bit to get in here."

"I'm sure, I'm sorry."

"You been out on the road some."

Gordon nodded. They were almost of a height, but Dock was twice as wide.

"You holding up?" Dock let go, and surveyed his face. "Eating?"

"Some."

"Sleeping?"

"Some."

"Want me to pick up a customer or two you have out of town?"

"Nah," he said.

Dock nodded. "OK. Look, no pressure, Gordon, but Annie and I talked all this through with your mother."

"I know."

"If you want to stay, you should stay. But if I were you I'd follow that girl. She knows where she's headed, and she's not bad-looking company."

Gordon laughed and touched his forehead. Emery laughed and touched his forehead.

There were two unfinished projects on the floor out back: a spray rig and double tilt utility trailer.

"So tell me what's happening in the shop these days." Dock stepped inside. "But consider yourself warned," he said, as Emery overtook him and pulled on his welding helmet. "This boy is full of beans. I mean he ate three cans of pinto beans last night." Dock mimicked a man eating beans out of a can, circling an imaginary spoon in his fist from can to mouth. "Safety hazard. Keep him away from the torches."

"Ha," Gordon said. "Thanks for the tip." Emery laughed again and drew back his lips to show them his teeth, like a wild animal. They stood in the cool space, the smell of burnt minerals and cleaning fluid sharp in their nostrils.

Dock told Gordon that other than a few passes on scrap metal with stick electrode, and the couple of minor projects he had watched John do and assisted with, he hadn't done much more. Gordon told him it had to be five hundred more than a few passes, and that Dock had learned more than he realized while working on the single engine stand.

"It's still in working order, isn't it?"

"It's pretty solid," Dock admitted, his cheeks red.

"That was all you. I saw every piece of it. I was right back there," Gordon said, and together they said, "working on the disc cultivator." It'd come in rusted pieces like a bolt's worth of moth-eaten reddish brown fabric—a never-ending project to restore.

They stood beside each other looking out of the shop toward the Gas & Grocer.

"So how long do we have you, young Walker?"

"A few days," Gordon said. "If I go."

"Don't get started on me," he said. "You're going."

"I'm thinking about it."

"Whatever you need to be here for, you can do a little less often."

"I guess that's right."

"What am I supposed to do all day every day if you don't go? Isn't enough work for two men."

"You've got me there," Gordon said. "I know you're up for the work."

"We all love your mother, Gordon. You know that, right?"

"I know."

"She won't be alone. Heck, May talked about hiring her on, just to get her out of the house a couple times a week. She'll need the help when Leigh's gone."

"I hadn't thought of that."

"Be good for her," he said. "Coffee?"

"We'd better."

Gordon filled the machine with water and scooped the grounds into the filter.

"You know, Gord," Dock said. "It'd mean the world to us to have a little steady work aside from alfalfa and hogs."

"I know it."

"Alfalfa's not great. Everything else is glutted. Wheat's too cheap."

"It's OK, Dock." He wanted Dock to stop talking.

"I know you think you have responsibilities around here." He nodded out the window toward the horizon, and held up a hand. "Hear me out. Try it for a year. It's only a few hours away. You can come back whenever you need to. Or if I get stuck. You've got a good truck right?"

They laughed at that. That truck had had four transmissions in its five-hundred-thousand-mile life.

"Would give us a year to save a little from whatever work comes through here to get Annie and Emery back to her family in Kansas."

"You'd go?" Gordon looked stricken.

"Here you were thinking you had to hold the town together like your father did, but the town's disappeared on you," Dock said. "You're free." He extended a hand, and Gordon gave him his own, and they shook. Dock's face broke open in a smile of relief. "Boy howdy," he said, "am I ever going to have Leigh Ransom on my good side. Guess who's getting free peach pie for the next couple days before she leaves?"

Gordon handed Dock a coffee mug, and they looked outside. The morning was yellow and sere. Horseflies glinted over the browning turf and thick, needled weeds.

"Not much left to it, is there?" Dock said. All they could see from where they stood was the closed Gas & Grocer, one broken window and its lawn already overgrown with thistle. "Maybe it'll get a second wind."

"What'd you bring?" Gordon asked, looking at the trailer hitched to Dock's rig.

Outside Dock had some rusted-out lattice and a broken axle on a tractor trailer—parts for a refurbished ATV for Emery.

"New used."

Dock nodded. "You got it."

"You know what Dad would've said."

"'That's a good man.'"

They both laughed.

"Be expensive to do?" Dock asked.

"Only if you charge yourself. You'll be the one doing it." Both of these sentences were John Walker's, verbatim, and Dock wanted to laugh but Gordon was serious. "Whatever you can't find in the scrap metal pile we'll have to purchase, and then there's the cost of the electricity."

"That'll be it?"

Gordon nodded.

"How do we start?"

"Prep and clean up. That'll take a full day."

"Like your father."

"Yes, sir. What do we need from the back?"

"Metal." He grinned sheepishly.

"But what kind?"

"You're not going to tell me."

"You start. Any ideas you have."

"Can we reinforce the ramps with angle iron?"

"We could."

"But," Dock considered, watching Gordon's face, "rectangular tubing is stronger. Do the job right."

Gordon nodded. "What else?"

"We'll need enough plate for fenders."

"Quarter inch?"

Dock stooped down and felt the ramp hangars. "Quarter inch here," he said. "Eighth inch for the fenders."

"Let's go check the scrap," Gordon said. "See what we've got."

The pile was out back in a circle of blinding sun. A sheet of metal so rusted it looked like copper-colored eyelet; sections of cemetery gate; curled edges of warped, corrugated steel; a bicycle wheel; six bicycle frames and four spools of wire and railroad spikes, chain-link, two bulldozer buckets, hubcaps, trash bins, iron piping, steel piping. The pile was twelve feet wide and organized by metal and by function but still half as many feet high. Bright, upright stacks of sheet metal like mirrors flashed in the daylight and they held their forearms up against their eyes.

"He never threw anything away," Gordon said.

Dock nodded at the pile. "Think we can use that?" He picked up a sheet of low carbon steel and miller moths lifted from beneath its shadow and batted softly against their faces and shirts.

"Perfect. How are you with a torch?" Gordon asked.

Dock unraveled the loops of gas hose and turned on the acetylene, then the oxygen. He checked the pressure, tapped the regulators with his index finger, and Gordon pointed to the wall. Dock retrieved two face shields and began again. He cracked open the valve on the torch, spark-lit the acetylene, and black smoke woofed up between the two men. He slowly cracked the oxygen to make the flame cleaner and shorter, and the smoke disappeared. The torch had its own distinctive roar. As he adjusted the oxygen down several blue points of flame jetted from the torch nozzle. When they were tight against the nozzle, the torch was ready to cut.

"Now let's turn it off," Gordon said, "and clean up some rust. You need to grind that area smooth and remove the paint from the area where we'll have to weld. First job is always to prepare the joint—no rust, no paint, no dirt."

"God help me, I know. But when we *do* start welding?" Dock returned to the torch and stepped toward the machine.

Gordon nodded. "Go ahead. Show me. Check your connections."

"Check."

Dock showed him: socks pulled up beneath his pants, which came down over the tops of his boots. Sleeves rolled down. Helmet on, hood lifted for the time being. He pointed to the lifted shop door. Ventilation. Dock pointed to the ground beneath his feet. Dry. He turned and showed Gordon his back pocket: work-duty gloves, ready to go.

"God," Gordon laughed. "Where was I when you learned the routine?"

"School," Dock smiled. "He put me through the wringer. Once I poured water over a couple spot welds on a broken johnny bar and I thought he was going to punch me in the gut."

"You poured water on them? Mid-project?"

Dock winced. "Alright, alright. I know."

"OK, next. What's your material?"

"Gordon. You remind me so much of your dad."

"OK."

"Don't feel bad about going. It's the only choice," he said. "And you know I'll need you. There'll be a long line of customers with money in their hands, right?"

"Sure, Dock."

"And I'll call on you."

*   *   *

That night in the factory Gordon told Leigh about the morning with Dock, and that he'd get his things together. He was leaning against the brick wall and she took her place in his arms, her head against his chest, and took his hand in hers.

"Aren't you happy?" he said.

"Yes," she answered, but was surprised not to feel anything as she said it. It used to be that her words created the feeling they described. Now she sensed the gap between the two, and wondered if it'd always been there. She wasn't sure what she felt. "And you?"

He was quiet a full minute. "Happy." He bumped his tennis shoe against hers.

Tonight he was a mile farther behind that line he'd never let her cross, had never crossed for her. When she closed her eyes, she couldn't picture his face. Something else had claimed him. She thought maybe they could still outrun it.

Before coming West the Walkers were camped briefly in a northeast Atlantic state, in a small town with verdant rolling hills, clear lakes, moss-covered barns, and hardwood trees with wide, flat-leafed blades that grew big as wet green hands. There, each man at his turn sweated before a rock slab hearth, shaping and twisting red-hot steel with a four-pound hammer on a heavy cast anvil. Some thousands of years before that, they were watchmen gathered high on a windswept moor beneath a spray of stars, sitting late into the night around a fire hemmed in by a ring of stones. Long after the women and most of the men had gone to sleep, and the constellations had tilted above them, and all the nocturnal creatures and insects clicking and whirring in the brush had fallen silent, their bellies filled with blood and feather and bone, these old Walkers stared into the flames as minerals began to shine and liquify in the rock, and they knew just what to do. It was a discovery they would not have made had they not been sentinels of a kind, and each Walker in his time relayed the message to his son: the metalwork should ever afterward remind them of this duty. And so in the midst of the hundreds of wars that followed, and during years upon years as migrants among the hungry and hopeless, they would have learned that compassion is fearless and unthinking, or it's not compassion.

Lamar Boggs was only a young man, they say, when his companions left him for dead. He was just starting out in the world, visiting his older brother who had been trading out West for a decade. There were many like him, eager for their chance at adventure and fortune. His party was a small group of neighbors and distant cousins, all of them hoping to find some measure of freedom they felt unavailable in their hometowns. They were doing as their own forefathers had done: helping themselves. It was a virtue. They traveled hundreds of miles together, became as brothers. Traded shoes and knives, boiled coffee, gutted antelope and sliced the meat thin enough to dry smoke on sticks around their campfires. Among them were a few young women, one of them an Elizabeth with strawberry blonde hair who cast Boggs long looks and smiled shyly. Once, he helped her into the wagon, taking her hand and the back of her arm. She smelled, he thought, like butterscotch. He'd had it once. No matter where he was in the group, a dozen miles ahead, or beside the wagon, or five miles behind, he knew exactly where he was in relation to her.

He would not be able to recall what happened late one afternoon that left him on his back, his vision dark, and the men he'd been riding with circling around him in the increasing snow, looking down, talking it over, their coats pulled tight to their throats. He looked up at them and felt the ground moving beneath him. It was as if a giant wheel had been set turning— everyone had set it turning, he had set it turning—and now it would have to spin itself out. The weather was bad, the fort seventeen miles farther on, and now—certainly he had been shot—there was reason to believe there were enemies afoot. Boggs knew there was none among them with room on their horses, and there was no room in the wagon. That his own horse must be down, too, or they would've strapped him to it. Surely they would have strapped him to it. One by one in the snow the men turned away. Perhaps they thought he was already dead. He could not speak or move in protest. He listened instead for the sound of the young woman's protest, but it did not come. He knew he was bleeding into the snow. Many men and women as undeserving of the fate had bled into this same ground, he knew. He had not thought he'd be one of them. As his grandfather had once told him in his parlor in St. Louis, every empire has its price.

As everyone understood it, and as John Walker had himself once confirmed, the first Walker came West just after the Civil War. He was a quiet, dark-eyed man, as all the Walkers were, and knew almost nothing of hunting, especially not in this region. He was a metalworker and a wheelwright and had done only a little bird shooting for sport: doves, sage grouse, pheasant. The land would've been sparsely populated back then, and cold on the day in question. Nevertheless, he'd decide to head out across the plain looking for someone to trade with for meat. He had a wife and a son, and it would be their first winter there, and there were hundreds of pounds of red meat, he'd heard, in a single kill of moose or elk. Someone would trade him.

Say he turned off a narrow track that wound over a lace of fresh white snow along a river. This is just past the BLM road, ten, fifteen miles north, near Horses. You take the road off the highway about twelve miles, then east for three miles. Then north again. *Way* up there. That's where he'd have been.

There would've been tracks of other carts. There wouldn't have been any threats other than failing light and increasing cold. By this particular night in this particular winter, the country would have long been broken.

This Walker would not have been worried, as he traveled, and what he'd find is the kind of thing you find exactly when you are not worried, when you are relaxed and warm enough to believe that no real harm can come to you. Behind the clouds, the sun—or possibly the moon—was high over the rim of the plain. There, in the vast white page before him, he'd see a small heap that at first sight could have been an animal—possum or even polecat, some poor creature to eviscerate and fry up and eat.

Suddenly he'd rush in, racing over the frozen ground with his open coat flapping like wings. There was Boggs, bleeding in the snow, a red slush around him. He would not have been able to speak.

Walker would've dragged him home on his sled—a sick and dying man instead of meat for his family—and as he pulled the sled through a stand of homesteads, the people of Lions would've looked out at them both. Boggs would've been filthy, his hair dark and shaggy, rings around his eyes, and dressed as if from a different era. A horrible stench. Those passing by outside would've put their hands over their mouths and turned away.

Walker was bringing this man home, to his family?

To his wife and son?

What was the matter with the man? Tend him out here, set him up in the stable, for God's sake. He could be sick. He'd get every last one of them sick.

In the weeks to come, no one would come for him, no one would claim him.

How was it that he had simply appeared in the snow like that?

And wounded like that?

He could only have been alone and running from something. No one would just leave him.

If they had, they weren't good people.

And who would've traveled among such men?

He'd bring them all bad luck.

He was a drunk, or a thief, or worse.

Likely he was being pursued. Now his pursuers would bear down on Lions, on their own homes.

Give him some water, give him some bandages, and set him on his way.

They couldn't have exactly said why this man gave them the horrors, but he did. After several weeks, Walker would finally have been convinced to take the poor man out of town to protect his own family—and to protect Boggs himself. The young man would've still been recovering, still weak. They'd have gone together on horseback up country and built a small hut of timber and earth with a floor of hardpacked dirt. For all its ruggedness, remarkably straight.

In all the years to come the young man who lived there would remain unchanged. He'd wear the same mended shirt and blackened rabbit skin leggings he'd coveted as rugged and wild when he first left St. Louis. He wouldn't mind the cold, or the heat. Walker would bring him cloth, needles, thread, coffee and sugar, blankets, some flints and steel, and small tools and promise to return after a week or two with more food. When he did return, with rabbits and sage hens, the young man ate everything before him and wanted only to know that Walker would come again.

There's a radiance to the edges of each blade of grass up there on that mesa. A hardness to every line. Wind jerks the stains of clouds over the ground like apparitions in a magic lantern slide, and if you were to pass by, you might see a pair of white hands pressed against the glass of the hut's single window and the white circle of a face looking out, waiting.

Leigh and Gordon left home in the old truck, their things packed on a small trailer and in the bed, blue tarps neatly cinched down over all of it.

"They'll stop and ticket you if you don't tie it down real well," he said, circling the bed and checking each taut hitch.

There's a photograph of them from their last night together in Lions that Georgianna kept pinned to her refrigerator for years. It's evening in the photograph, late summer. Leigh is barefoot in a pair of Gordon's jeans that she cut off into shorts, with a red bandana tied over her hair. She's sitting on the stoop in front of the Walkers' old white house, next to Georgianna, who's in her long cotton yellow sundress and one of John's old shirts, and has her arm around Leigh, face turned to her. Leigh has both fists beneath her chin, elbows propped on her brown knees. In the foreground, to the left, Gordon is carrying a box of her clothes. He's looking past May, who took the photograph, as if there were someone or something just behind her. His expression is one of intelligence and calm. If you were holding the photograph in your hand, he'd be looking right over your shoulder.

In the truck, on the way, there was a weight and a tightness in the silence between them. They held hands briefly, twice, their interlaced fingers resting in the space between the driver and passenger side seats where even a season ago she would have been sitting. The first time Gordon disengaged his hand to turn the radio station, and the second time Leigh pulled hers away.

The truck scattered desert light as they sped over the highway. The grass thinned out as the plain beneath them rose. Pleated and wrinkled, the golden ground unrolled in an unmarked parchment around them. Outside the windshield, a tiny, empty grain elevator jackknifed against the sky, which was a perfect heartache blue. They'd rolled their windows down and the air outside was hot as smoke and the loose daylight and dust made their eyes fill with tears.

"I thought I'd feel freer."

"We're not even halfway there."

She turned the radio off, then on again, and scanned. Country songs. Commercials. She turned it off. "Are there any radio stations up there?"

"Up where?"

"Where you go."

"It's not like I drive to the moon."

"Why didn't you ever take me?"

He gave her a look of surprise. "You'd want to go?"

"Not really."

He said nothing.

"I didn't think it would be like this," she said. "This summer. This drive to college."

"Me either."

"I guess I have to forgive your shitty behavior."

Gordon glanced at her a moment, then focused on the road before him. "Guess I have to forgive yours."

Five miles outside of the city, when the traffic increased and the highway widened, Leigh made him stop at a Walmart, where she bought a blue and white polka-dot dress that flared out from her waist, and glitter for the backs of her wrists, and earrings of looped silver wire. She bought soap and lotion and a caddy for the shower, and new underwear and three T-shirts, new sheets, two towels and three scented candles. Gordon waited in the café, where he drank a cup of black coffee and made funny faces across his table to a child in the adjacent booth. When she was finished shopping, he waited for her outside while she changed in the bathroom.

"Very nice," he said when she had lifted her bags in the cab of the truck and turned for him in her polka dots. "But I like you in your regular clothes."

"Don't be a party pooper," she said. "Don't you need anything?"

"I'm good." They climbed in the truck and he pulled out of the parking lot back onto the road.

"Don't you want anything?"

"I'm good."

"Hungry?"

"Eh."

"Let's go somewhere good. I'll buy."

He lifted one of the foiled-wrapped sandwiches May had given them. "We have these."

Leigh took them and one at a time threw them out the window.

"Hey," he said. "I could get a ticket for that."

"You and your tickets."

"They're perfectly good sandwiches."

"This from the guy who eats cheese and tomato sandwiches from the gas station outside of Burnsville."

"It's food. It shouldn't be wasted."

She reached over and pinched the back of his upper arm. "Oh, lighten up a little."

"You got to tell me how to do that."

They glanced at each other and laughed. He took her hand.

Leigh found the city an almost unbelievable solace. They pulled into town by late afternoon along a narrow, busy street with long lawns of green and blue velvet and sprinklers and fountains and entire blocks of brick and painted houses and landscaped yards. All that hot summer in Lions and here were thick white beds of impatiens and window boxes of bright green geraniums. Huge canopies of imported oak trees and maple trees, alder and aspen and ash. There was no white glare, none of the human dust of home. There were pubs and cafés and restaurants and bars and farmers' markets and grocery stores and co-ops and art galleries and somehow, in its design to address her every need, it placed her at the center of the world, in the middle of every room.

"Park somewhere," she said.

"We have to unload this stuff."

"Come on," she took his arm. "No one's going to take anything."

He shook his head—no short cuts—and drove toward campus where they found her dormitory and he helped her unload everything into her room. Her roommate, a young woman from Pueblo, had not yet arrived. Gordon hauled in the few crates and boxes of Leigh's things while she unpacked them in the room.

He hung every picture straight, moved the dresser where she asked him to, turned the bed so her body would lie lengthwise against the windows, as it had at home.

"Your turn?" she asked, collapsing in a dorm-issued armchair.

"You don't have to help."

"Meet me somewhere then. I'm going to walk through town."

Outside, the sun lowered and the shadows lengthened and the beauty of the day deepened. She went everywhere, stepped inside every store. Touched dresses, smelled perfumed oils, smiled broadly at the young women working behind the registers. Here it finally was. People smiled back at her. Young men said hello. Somewhere in her mind was Lions—hollow, bare, too bright to see, each building and familiar house and barn obliterated behind a burst of blinding sun. The very name of the place an echo on empty plain.

A couple hours, one fizzy lemon drink, a pair of sandals and two silk scarves later she found Gordon in his room. It was on the opposite side of campus from her own—oddly far away after living a hundred feet apart from him all her life—in a small, brick building of four floors. Nothing like the massive tower she'd been assigned to. His roommate, an Emerson Perez, had at the last minute arranged to live off campus and left Gordon without any company. This meant he had two narrow rooms to himself; in one, a long, metal-framed twin bed, where he slept, and in the other, John's old armchair he'd unloaded and set up as if it were the Walkers' old living room. Next to it, the Naugahyde chair that had come in the dorm room. He hung a spider plant in a pot that Leigh had made as a girl, and given to John on Father's Day, over which she recalled Georgianna and May exchanging a wink and, on May's part, a deep laugh. Also on this side of the room Gordon unfolded the brown, orange, and mustard-colored afghan that Georgianna had crocheted herself and which had been on the couch at home. He set up John's books in half a dozen neat stacks beside his chair, the binoculars from the shop alongside the books.

Leigh stepped into his room and saw all of it.

He sat in the old chair with his hands spread open on its arms and smiled at her across the dimly lit room.

"What do you think?"

"I—don't know what to say."

"Don't look like that," he said. "Who else's stuff could I have brought? Come on, Leigh. I don't have all the tip money saved that you have, for new stuff."

"I guess."

"Mom told me to bring whatever I needed."

"No," she said. "I know."

"Sit down."

"It's still light. There's live music downtown. I have to go to the grocery store."

"Can't we just sit here together in the quiet for a little? Half an hour?"

So she sat in the dorm chair beside John Walker's chair and Gordon poured them each a shot of whiskey. She looked across the soccer field outside Gordon's building at a handful of young men passing a ball and running up and down the field. On the far side, a trio of girls in bright T-shirts walked arm in arm in arm toward a street packed with bicycles and cars. Tricked-out pickup trucks paraded in endless loops. All the lawns were thick and soft.

After they finished their whiskeys she convinced Gordon to drive her to the overbright, overstuffed grocery, but afterward he insisted on going back to his dorm.

"You just want to sit in your room?"

He shrugged. "Tired, I guess."

"Everything you could possibly want or need is here, Gordon."

"Need for what?"

It seemed to Leigh over the course of the next two days, then three, that Gordon was being perversely obstinate, and she began to feel a vague distaste—an involuntary aversion—to everything in him that reminded her of John Walker or of home: his old shirts, the smell of Lava soap, the slow, careful, almost stupid look on his face when he was introduced to someone, or considering something new before him. The silence when others greeted him cheerfully, asked him how he liked it here, asked him how he was.

"Don't you think about how people might see you?"

"No."

"You should."

"Why? How do I look?"

It wasn't as though he were ignoring the physical world. He heard and saw things that escaped Leigh's attention—a long insect snapping its matchstick legs on the screen of a house they passed; a hawk above the soccer field diminished to a pinprick circling in the blue overhead; a whistling that came from a little yellow bird in the tree branches above them, which for Leigh had dissolved into the music of the restaurant speakers. He seemed sharper and older than he'd been in springtime, like a seasoned instrument both highly strung and perfectly tuned. But the effect of all this was disturbing. He was so quiet, and now so thin, and seemed to look not past the people and lights around him, but through them. He looked at Leigh as if he were not quite sure what she was. If the words between them had once been their map to the city on a hill—to the life they were going to make together here, and then later, when they'd graduated—Gordon was erasing each word, one at a time, as if his very existence described a vacancy.

In the next few days he accompanied Leigh around campus and through town, but whenever they met someone, or Leigh struck up a conversation—with a coffee barista, with the hostess at a restaurant where they had lunch—he seemed to retreat within himself. Everything he saw—girls in new blue jeans and bright T-shirts and jackets, the colored front windows of food co-ops and bistros and dress shops—seemed to feed the inclination. Every sentence he spoke terminated in a certain soft and low intonation meant to end the conversation. He'd cross his arms over his chest and look away, only just managing to avoid overt impoliteness. People noticed. They speak solely to her—they seemed not even to see him.

If on the next evening, and the evening after that, anyone had looked in the direction of his room from the athletic field, they would have seen his silhouette sitting behind closed curtains. Outside they laughed and slammed car doors. There was music on the green. It was a radio or it was a concert or it was a small student band. A little farther in the distance, behind a line of trees, it was a crowded bar with swings instead of bar stools. They were on their way to somewhere they could dance, knowing what the day was worth and how much they had to spend and digging in their pockets for every last penny while he sat inside in his chair. Sunlight galloped past his window. The moon rose. The stars marched overhead.

Every afternoon of the first week of classes Leigh found him there, in his room. She began to notice none of his things had moved on his desk—his toothbrush, his backpack, his calculus book—from the day before.

Three weeks into classes, she found him in John's old chair finishing a Western that was falling apart in his hands, and already on his second whiskey, which, like his father, he took slowly. His unmade bed. His unchanged clothes.

"It's like you're not even here, Gordon."

"I'm right here."

"It's like you're not even trying."

"Leigh," he said. "Please. Be patient with me."

"You shouldn't be doing this," she said, and gestured around them. "It's no help."

"I should be going out."

"Yes."

"Making plans."

"Yes."

"Having fun."

"Yes."

Her face was flushed and she stood and looked out the window. The girls were gone and the soccer players were gone. The grassy field was a soft navy blue.

"I'm not exactly feeling like myself," he said. "I guess it's not what you had in mind."

She took a breath and turned back to him. "What are you reading?"

He held it up. "Dad read it to me once when I was sick. It took me forever to find it." It was held together by a rubber band. The red-eyed horse rearing, the man in the duster, the coiled snake, the beautiful woman wrapped in turquoise ruffles. He closed the book and set it aside.

"Are you even leaving your room? Are you sick?"

"I'm fine."

"How was class today?"

He shrugged.

"Gordon." His eyes were glassy, and his teeth looked large—or like there were more of them than she'd remembered. Out in the hall a door opened, and the sound of music on a stereo swelled and faded as the same door slammed shut. "There's a city out there. Restaurants. Museums. A great big library. Two of them. Trees. Beautiful houses. Good people. Books to read. Good teachers. Kind people. Have you seen any of this? No. You don't want to see any of it."

"I guess you've got some of that right."

"You're not going to class," she said.

"Why do you say that?"

"I looked for you today."

"Why?"

"Because, stupid."

Outside in the hallway, the door opened again and the music flared to life.

"Gordon. Listen. It's 'Red River Valley.' What are the chances? Someone else is a throwback, too." She suddenly felt bright, felt the broad sun of home across her face and shoulders and she reached for his hand. "Come on, it's a sign. Let's dance."

"I don't want to dance."

"Come on, it's a sign!"

"Stop."

"Dance with me."

He pulled his hand away. "Leigh," he said sharply. "Please."

She sat and they were still, not talking, for a full minute.

"I'm sorry," he said. "I'm not being the best kind of man right now." He set his hands flat on his knees. "I'm not the best man right now."

"You don't have to say it twice."

"Please be patient."

"You already said."

He shook his head. "You go off so quickly," he said softly. He looked up at her. "You went off so quickly."

She blushed and turned away. A moment later she put her hand on the side of his face, and brought her lips to his.

He pulled his face away.

Leigh crossed her arms and leaned back. "Something's wrong with you."

"Is it."

"I think you need help."

He said nothing.

"Like a counselor."

Nothing.

"I mean, for one, your parents." She waited.

He nodded once.

"And losing the shop. Moving away from home."

"I'm not losing the shop."

"OK."

"And I'll go back."

"Gordon."

They both pictured Lions then. The pigweed, foxtail, purslane, and countless unstoppable weeds in a spiny brown hide stretching from their front doors to the ditch on the side of the dusty road. All the stock barns collapsed in the weeds, rusted coils of pasture fences unspooled across the dirt. Jefferson Street, empty. Jorgensen's place, empty—the two-story white house that had always been lit up.

"Then won't you talk to someone?"

"You mean a psychologist."

"It comes with the tuition."

She watched him. He must have been imagining what he'd say to such a person. That he'd discovered or been given a new job in life, one he neither wanted nor didn't want, but which he was compelled to perform.

"And if you don't do it," this doctor would ask, "what happens?"

"I was born to do it."

"And you recently lost your father?"

"Yes, sir."

The doctor would nod at that. Jot something down. Interesting, he might think.

To ignore this task his father gave him on his deathbed, Gordon would explain to the counselor, would be to live a lie. To do it, however, would be to turn his back on everyone and everything he once thought was his life.

"A very pleasant life," Gordon would explain. "That was supposed to include Leigh. And clean and simple rooms in a clean and simple house in a clean and simple town."

"That doesn't sound so indulgent."

"I didn't say I'd be turning my back on indulgence. I'd be turning my back on a certain kind of life. A very good kind of life."

"Does she know about this—job—of yours?"

"She knew my father."

"But you haven't spoken of it?"

"Not explicitly."

"Why not?"

"She might think I was crazy."

"She thought your father was?"

"A lot of people did."

"Do you think," the doctor would ask slowly, "that *I* think you're crazy?"

"Yes."

"Does thinking so change your feelings about this—task, as you call it?"

"No."

Then Gordon would describe the hut where the wounded man lived, the alternative to the pleasant, airy, sunny home he might have shared with Leigh.

"It's a way to feel close to your father?"

"I guess."

And this doctor would nod, and refer to his notes, and respond in kind with a prescription.

In Gordon's dorm room, Leigh sat forward in the extra chair and closed her eyes, then suddenly stood up. Somewhere in the distance the sound of a crackling motorcycle rose in the late summer sky.

"Stay here with me," he said.

"I need some air."

"I know we've been having a hard time," he said. "Leigh, look at me."

"You won't tell me what's going on."

"It's all falling apart," he said.

"That's it? That's all you have to say?"

He shook his head. "What do you want me to say?"

"I mean what is this?" She gestured at his chair, the afghan. The room he'd created.

"I thought we could get a fresh start again out here," he said.

She looked around his room in disbelief. "You did?"

"I'm talking about you and me. I thought it could be like it was at home again. That we could start over from how it was, before."

"No, Gordon. That would be like starting over from a negative number. Do you understand? I don't want things to be like they were at home."

"You don't."

"For God's sakes no. Why did I come here?" She flung her hand at the shade he'd pulled down over one window and knocked it sideways. As it swung slowly still, it dawned on her. "You only came to try to lure me back."

He shook his head. "No, Leigh."

"That's exactly what this is. You were never going to stay."

"Listen."

"You were going to lure me back." She said it this time quietly, as if to herself.

Gordon fixed his eyes on the line where the wall met the carpet.

"I am not going back in any way, shape, or form."

"I just need a little time there. Six months. A year."

"I don't want to be there and I don't want things to be like they were there and I don't want to be any place like it. Not for a day and definitely not for a year."

"OK, Leigh."

"I'm not going to be like your mother."

"OK."

"Good." Her breath was shallow and her heart raced high in her chest. "I'm going now."

"OK."

She went from his dorm into town to meet her roommate and a few other new friends at a café where you could sometimes convince them to sell you a glass of beer. There was a quartet of young men from the college playing from the Great American Songbook, and she and her friends took up the ragged love seat and armchairs in a circle around a gas fireplace. The evening was just cool enough for it. Someone, somehow, procured a bottle of wine, and they filled their empty coffee cups and chatted and listened to the music. But even in his absence Gordon managed to ruin the night. When the wine was gone and the young men were packing up their instruments, she crossed campus. It was well after midnight, and quiet, just the sound now and then of a lone car on the main strip and the sprinklers ticking over the blue lawns and early autumn flowers. She followed the sidewalk toward Gordon's dorm.

The door to his building was locked, and her own ID card didn't work. She pressed her forehead a moment against the metal door, then straightened and walked over the damp grass to his window. It was on the first floor, but a good ten feet from the ground. She scanned the immaculate grass for something to throw at it. A piece of gravel. Nothing. She sat with her back against the brick building, facing the lawn, her head and arms in a pile on her knees. When the first birds called out from the line of tall, narrow poplars and the illuminated sky in the east began blanking out the stars, she raised her hands and spread her fingers and carefully, as the woman at the Lucy Graves had done, closed the dark empty space above her head like the petals of a flower.

Around dawn someone opened the door to Gordon's building from the inside, and she went in. She could see his door open from the end of the hall as she approached. He's in the bathroom, he thought. I'll take him to breakfast. We'll go somewhere pleasant. She told herself how it would be with each step of her feet until she stood before the empty room. He was gone, and he'd taken everything with him.

Gordon drove east as the moon set, hands trembling on the wheel as he shuddered in the cold truck. He'd rolled down the windows to let the cold in and keep himself awake. He drove as night dissolved around him. The sun came up and he entered Lions and knew all of it—what it smelled like, and what time the birds woke—as well as he knew his own body. It was early autumn, the grass and weeds an endless span of cool blonde parchment.

Before the summer, the world and all its forms seemed made for pleasure and consolation. His shadow printed on the street outside the diner. Rain against the window. A train of two hundred heavy, black, silent cars pushing west in slow motion. That world was lost to him now—and yet he'd never felt so awake.

So life was sweet only where it was also bitter. He would take it all, without condition, without reservation, and without wishing it were otherwise. Not because he was virtuous or good, but because he was tired, his hands were empty, and he had no energy in him to be otherwise. The world vibrated around him. There wasn't much in it he felt was worth chasing.

The shop would be there, just ahead off the highway, beside his house, and in its way that was everything. His father had shown Gordon that in the undivided heart there lives a secret love bringing a man to silence beyond all thought, teaching him to repudiate and disavow all that is false in the world. Gordon would go back to the work.

There were no lights on in town. The diner wasn't open yet. Boyd's was dark. He pulled over in front of the empty hardware store and looked over the dusty junk in the store window. Chintzy vases and teacups and saucers with roses and lilies and forget-me-nots painted in ribbons around gilded rims. Board games—Connect Four, Donald the Donkey, and Lose All You Have, the colored boxes faded, the shrinkwrapped plastic brown with dust.

He drove the length of town, and down the side street where the backhoe service shop had been when he was a boy, and from there, along a dirt road. Dock and Annie's place made him stop in his tracks. The east side blackened and a dark smoky stain rising up the face. The staves buckling. The windows broken and glass shards glittering in a pile of dark blue ashes. Emery.

With a lighter or a book of matches. Gordon could see it. Emery would have been alone in the living room. Annie in the kitchen shaking cubed beef and white flour in a plastic grocery bag. Dock would have been out back among the pigs, kicking them gently with his old, flat, brown boots away from the gate and holding the heavy bucket overhead.

He drove farther down the frontage road toward his house, parked the truck, and got out. He put his hands in his pockets and shrugged his shoulders against the cold. There was a light on in his house, and before the window at the kitchen sink, May Ransom was filling the teakettle. Upstairs, the fainter yellow window of his room, where his mother had slept all summer.

Dock was in the shop. Inside, behind the tiny side window, he and his family were gathered. There was a little table set up that Gordon recognized as an end table from his own home, and Annie was slicing something on her plate, and Emery had his head back, roaring. Gordon could see his huge, milk-white teeth through the glass. It was early breakfast time.

So they were living in the shop now.

Well, it was cold out, and getting colder—a family needed a warm place. And it was true that Dock needed whatever extra work he could get, and that Gordon had turned it all over to him. Gordon stood outside the shop looking in. His eyes burned. He was glad they had it. He knew they'd take care of it and use it well. He turned back toward the old blue truck. He'd keep driving this morning. He could come back down here and see his mother in a few days.

"It's punishment, this heat," Dock said and took his seat at the counter. He was the first customer and the Lucy Graves was clean and quiet. May turned over a mug for him and filled it with black coffee. "That's what Annie says. Still hitting ninety and coming up on October."

"Annie ought to know better." May extended a menu and he pointed at the blackboard breakfast special and she set the menu back on its stack. "It's always been a desert."

"And it's cursed," he said, nodding at her for emphasis.

"Oh, Dock, not you, too."

"The sun wants to kill you, for one."

"It's a desert." She turned on the griddle.

"It feels personal."

"It isn't personal. This is the country we live in."

"How do you do that?"

"What, poach an egg? You put vinegar in the water, then you stir it fast when it gets hot." She opened an egg with one hand and dropped it into the pot.

"What does that do? The vinegar?"

She shrugged. "It poaches the egg." He watched her as she stirred and used a slotted metal spoon to gently lift the poached egg out of the water. She set it over some sliced ham on an English muffin. "You have any work?"

He rotated the plate before him and reached for the pepper. "Only because it's John's place. Once word gets out that the Walkers are gone, they'll take their jobs to Sterling, or Greeley, or wherever else they go. There's a place in Severance. They'll drive out there."

"You don't give yourself enough credit."

"It's not about me," he said. "I could be anyone. It's about John and Gordon. How good they were. You think Gordon will come back?"

"I hope not."

He nodded, chewing. "For my sake, I hope he doesn't come back till we fix the house."

"I imagine that shop is pretty right and tight," May said.

"Tell the truth, I prefer it to the house we had."

"I'm sure Annie doesn't feel that way."

"No," Dock said. "It's hard on her." He shook his head. "God, this is good. What's in that sauce?"

"Butter."

When Boyd came in at the end of the day, he echoed Dock.

"Something wrong with this whole place." He filled a glass of water for himself as May wiped down the tables one last time. "Probably always has been." He opened the cooler and took out the sandwich she'd set aside for him. "We've been here eight years together. Leigh's gone. Let's get out."

"And go where, Boyd?"

"Burnsville. Open a bigger place. Restaurant-pub combined."

"You're not half as imaginative as Leigh. Don't you want to move to California? A little seaside town somewhere?"

"Well, give me some credit, Maybelline." He unwrapped the sandwich, peeling open the bread to peek inside, and sat at the counter. "I guess I've moved around some."

"I know it."

"When I was a kid," he said, "I used to read about this big swath from Nebraska through Colorado to New Mexico," he said. "Trappers. Traders. Indians. Spanish, French, Russian, Chinese."

"Yeah?"

"So much blood. Had this big gray book with orange lettering on the cover. Used to read through my fingers," he said, "the stories were that gruesome." He took a bite of the sandwich. "And I was a teenaged boy. I didn't get squeamish easy."

"Huh," May said, and set out stacks of lunch meat to thaw for the next day.

"The scalping and hacking and butchering. The things they did with their—"

May put up her hand. "OK," she said, "I get it."

"And all of that for what?" He took a napkin from the dispenser. "My bar? Your diner? A Gas & Grocer?" He shook his head.

"How is Burnsville any different?"

He counted off the names of its business establishments. Taco Bell, Motel 6, Perkins, Ponderosa Grill, the good Italian place, the reservoir.

"Oh, Burnsville," she said. "Oh, you shining city on a hill." He grabbed her by the arm as she passed behind him and he spun her around and smacked her bottom. She laughed. "Oh, you beacon of hope for all the world."

"You have a real attitude problem," he said. "You know that?"

"Let's get out of here. Been cooped up all day." Just as she said so, a woman knocked on the locked door, shielded her eyes with her hand and peered in. They could hear her muted call of hello through the glass. There was a white minivan parked in front of the bar. May unlocked the diner door and the woman stepped back as she pushed it open.

"How can I find the man who owns that bar?" she asked. She was tall and gaunt and had long, dark hair that hung down to her waist, and circles around her eyes. May froze and her stomach went cold.

"You got him," Boyd said, circling up behind May. "Need a cold one? Should be open. Just came over here to get a sandwich."

"I'm the sister of the man who drowned in your water tower." She reached into her coat pocket and took out a white sheet of paper. A copy of the newspaper story out of Greeley.

"Oh, dear God," May said.

"When I saw about the dog," she said, and her voice broke, "I knew."

Inside the diner, she would not sit. Boyd instinctively went behind the lunch counter and crossed his arms. May turned on the orange overhead lights and took a stool.

"Coffee?"

"No."

"Did you drive all the way from Pennsylvania?"

Behind the counter on the freezer was a copy of the same newspaper article, held up with a magnet for the highway clientele following the sign for the living ghost town. The woman was staring at it.

"What kind of people hang something like that on the wall?"

Boyd turned and looked at it. Mystery man in a ghost town, it read. Spirits trapped in the walls of the bar. Ghost of a ghost, it read: the last recorded instance of a man drowning himself in a well or water tower in Lions was in 1923. That man, gone nearly a century ago, fit the same description as the recent wanderer, it read. Many residents admitted to being spooked by the coincidence.

"He wasn't a ghost of a ghost," the woman said. "He was my brother."

"I'm sorry," May said, red-faced. "We're so sorry." The woman nodded, raised a hand at May. Her eyes shone with tears. May walked around to the woman's side of the counter and took her arm. "Won't you please sit, please?" But the woman did not want to sit.

"Ah," Boyd said, and shook his head. He touched the scar on his face, and looked out across the street at the bar window, which was still cracked.

"That dog was all he had left. She was all he had left."

"We didn't know anything about him," May said. "We're so sorry."

"What happened?" The woman looked from May to Boyd and back again, her eyes wide. "Do you know what happened?"

May folded her hands, her gaze fixed on a black shoe streak on the linoleum floor. For several minutes, no one spoke.

The woman put her face in her hands. May went behind the counter and called Chuck Garcia, watching as the woman slowly sat down cross-legged on the floor. It was Chuck's wife, Emily, who lifted her up off the floor. The woman wanted her brother's remains, she said, and the dog's.

"We're going to help you out," Chuck said, "whatever you need."

"I need a minute," she said. "I'm sorry, I didn't plan to—"

"It's alright," Emily said. She had pulled on a pair of blue jeans under a night shirt, her feet in sandals. "Come on. We'll take you home, get you some coffee."

Chuck and Emily took the woman outside and she followed them in her minivan back toward the frontage road and the Garcias' place. For several minutes Boyd and May sat side by side at the counter, not talking or moving.

"I feel sick," May finally said.

"Me, too."

"I think I want a beer."

Outside they crossed the street. Something fluttering caught her vision, and she turned to face the junk shop. "Marybeth?" she called, and waved her hand in the dark. Boyd came up beside her.

"Baby Jesus," he said. They glanced at each other, and rushed toward the rocking chair, where Marybeth Sharpe had expired in the afternoon heat earlier that day.

By lunchtime news of Marybeth's death and the stranger's visit had reached everyone remaining in town. Somehow Boyd seemed at the center of all of it, from early June to the night before.

"I heard one woman say you strangled her brother right here in the bar," Dock told him.

Boyd shook his head.

"Another guy says you went out in the street, the two of you."

Boyd nodded and folded the wipe cloth and hung it in his belt.

Dock laughed. "Most of them have the right of it though."

"What's that, Sterling? The story where I poured a beer on his head and forced him into jail for a night? The story where it's my fault the dog died, and the man killed himself, and drove everyone away?"

Dock raised a hand. "Sorry, Boyd," he said. "I meant no harm." He finished and paid for his beer and drove back to the shop.

Annie was in the kitchen pounding a steak in the bunkroom next to a cookstove Dock had bought at the camping store in Burnsville. She was weepy and put her head against Dock's chest.

"That poor old lady," Annie said. "We shouldn't have let her sit out there."

"She was a sweetie pie," Dock said. "And she was very old."

"Somebody should have checked in on her," Annie said. "I should have. You should have."

"I know it," he said, and stroked his wife's pale hair, still shining, still golden. "But it's OK how she went, too."

Annie nodded. "It is, isn't it?"

"Old lady loved that rocking chair."

They both laughed, and Annie took Dock's big fingers from her hair and kissed them.

Boyd called Chuck and asked him to remove the living ghost town signpost from the highway.

"That'll be the end of the Lucy Graves," Chuck said.

"We've had enough," Boyd told him, and truth be told, Chuck was glad to hear it. You go into the Lucy Graves, he thought, and you want there to be more than a diner, and maybe there is more, but all you have to study it by is the ordinary inventory of the place: the white plastic ramekins of club crackers, packets of sugar, the smell of heavy-duty cleaner with which May scrubbed the stainless steel. Lions was the same way. Maybe sometimes you even entertained the possibility of some of its wilder stories—at night, in the bar, when everybody got to talking. Lamar Boggs, for Pete's sake. But you should've known better. And when you thought back to the moments you wondered if it were true—Walker men tending a ghost up on the mesa—you should've felt pretty chastened. That's the word Chuck's grandfather would've used. People weren't interested in the regular, workaday truth, but that kind of truth was the real miracle, he thought, and looked at the hands at the ends of his arms. He opened and closed them.

People in Burnsville would ask Chuck all through the fall, and even in the winter, and over the years to come, who that man was who drowned himself in the water tower in Lions.

"I'm not at liberty to say," he would respond, regardless of the taunts and jabs from men like Boyd, or the remote politeness of a woman questioning him as Georgianna did. He respected the privacy of the man, and of his sister, who had requested it of him. And that, Chuck figured, was fair. You didn't always get—you almost never got—the whole story of every man, woman, or child who asked something of you in this world. What you got was the moment they stood before you. You'd have to take your chances, make your best judgment, and do whatever you were going to do. There was a sort of resolve you had to consult that went deeper than the facts of a man's personal history. At least, he came to think so.

Over the coming week, Leigh knew—she almost knew—that something wasn't right. But here was a man with golden brown eyes and a real smile. Something about him like a lighted window in the dark. Here were his friends—intelligent, wide-eyed, and full of good words. They expected nothing unreasonable of her beyond her company. They were easygoing, she thought, light-hearted. If she was sometimes vaguely aware of a soft, faraway drumbeat—a reminder or a decision to live her life in a different way—it would be there later just as well as now. Not yet, she felt in every step as she walked to class, as she planned the evening, or the next week, confident as she did so in the unfurling of her life in a clear and perfect direction toward the house and family and job that would at last fulfill the cumulative desires born of her impoverished life in Lions. Not yet. Not yet.

Tonight, here was a clear blue dusk, a cool evening in late September. Chairs set out in rings on a patio. Here were ten thousand small and pleasant reassuring whispers in the rustle of the trees. A string of colored lights was pinned in twenty neat parabolas up and down each side of the street from lamppost to lamppost, and here was a door that opened to the sidewalk, inside the ringing of silverware and human laughter and warmth, the small and perfect notes of rounded fingertips across piano keys, and this was how you ignored the very clear and very peculiar sense that everything making you feel good was the wrong thing.

She moved with her new friends from the patio to a house, from the house to an apartment, from the apartment to a dorm room. They walked as if there'd been no world before they were born, and there'd be no world left when—in a thousand years, happy, old, and perfectly content—they passed away.

She told them about the strange and gaunt tableland north of Lions, where the air was always the breath of winter, and the dirt was white as chalk. They sat in circles on dorm room rugs and in chairs and on the ends of twin beds. Everyone had a bottled beer. Everyone wore a beautiful sweater. Everyone had something to say about what they'd read the night before. Everyone was bumping their knee against someone else's, wetting their lips, smiling brightly.

For a minute or two, she had all their attention.

She told them about the wounded traveler who could walk barefoot and naked across a hundred miles of bone-breaking cold. And then all of John Walker's visits out of town, and Gordon's, and about Gordon's vow, and how he'd thrown his life away for the sake of something he wouldn't even talk about, not with anyone, not even with her. She hiccupped.

They stared at her. "Are you for real?" somebody said. He had dark shining hair and screwed up his face and raised an eyebrow.

"No no," somebody said, "I stopped there on my way out. It's true. It's all true. There's a sign on the side of the highway."

"That is the most asinine thing I've ever heard," somebody else said.

Someone changed the music. Someone handed Leigh a fresh beer.

"If that's true," somebody said, "you should totally go back." He flashed his eyes wide at everyone. "Ghost town."

"Nobody lives there anymore," Leigh said. "You can't live out there. Doesn't even have a grocery store. What are you supposed to eat? Bugs and dirt?"

Anyone still listening to her now was moving in close to bump a shoulder to hers, or to place a hand on her waist. They weren't that interested.

"I'm not going back," she said to no one. "I hate it there. Hate it." She felt the slight vibration of a passing train beneath her chair. The muted roaring of blood in her ears.

On her way home she passed a bright pub that smelled like beer and onions. Aprons of light poured out across the sidewalk from open doorways. Every small beautiful thing—the masses of green leaves, the way the interior lights from a restaurant lit up a line of blue glass bottles in its front window—seemed to shut a door on her. Not for you, it said. Not for you.

She found a little dive in what had once been a bank with a giant vault; it was nearly empty and quiet. No music, no TV. Gordon would have liked it. John, too. Only the murmur of human conversation. The ringing of glassware. At the bar she asked for something strong. The bartender was a young guy with a rough beard and a pair of suspenders over a white undershirt. He poured her four inches of amber liquid in a glass.

"You don't have your ID on you, do you?"

"Left it at home."

"Thought so," he nodded. "First one's on me," he said. "You look like your best friend just got hit by a train."

Boyd and May sat alone in the empty diner, stirring coffee, empty pie plates beside them. May had turned the overhead lights off and the front door was propped open. It was twilight, last day of September, and the evenings were finally cool again. Across the street, the bar was closed, the cracked window still boarded.

"We could move the bar in here," Boyd said, his elbows on the table and his head bent over the coffee cup. "Make it yours. Get a liquor license. Change the name of the place."

"No more Lucy Graves?"

"I think we should change it all."

"They're just windows, Boyd. We can fix them."

Boyd shrugged. His mustache had grown into an unkempt silver beard. "Maybe we ought to just go, too."

May shook her head. "I don't think I could get Georgie to leave, Boyd."

"You really mean to take care of her."

"I do."

"What about Annie?"

"Annie's got her hands full."

"These could be our last good years together, Maybelline."

"What, you want to be on vacation?" She was old enough to know better than to think of her life as dear just because it was hers. If where she had ended up was arbitrary, her partner just as much so, she loved and appreciated them no less for it. "I'm sorry," she said, and opened her hands. "I'm staying here. At my age you make a choice and you do it. Chuck will keep circling through town. Burnsville is there if we need it. Georgie needs me. Twenty-six years I've known her, she half raised my only child, and no doubt Leigh would have been all bad instead of half bad without the Walkers' help."

"OK," he whispered. He shook his head, staring into his mug.

She reached over and put a hand on his forearm. "Boyd. Come on."

He looked up, his blue eyes shining. "That man walked all that way. Somehow made his way. It wasn't until he got here—" He couldn't finish. His eyes spilled over and he pressed them with a forefinger and thumb.

"Boyd."

"You know something, May? I've wasted my life one night at a time, four beers in and trying to win people over. Some stupid joke. Some stupid story. Some stupid lie."

"Come on now."

May stood up and joined him on his side of the booth, and put her arm around him.

"I'm sick of the sound of my own voice."

"Well," she said, and nudged him, laughing softly.

"It's like I'm standing right beside myself all the time."

"Listen, Boyd. We were all responsible this summer. You didn't mean any real harm." She jostled him lightly. "Did you?"

He sniffed and sucked air in through his mouth and wiped his nose. "Seems like it started with me, doesn't it?"

"That's just people talking. Always been a place of big stories, hasn't it? You're only a man, Boyd. So you don't always get it right. Did you ever meet someone who did?"

He was quiet a minute. "John Walker. Didn't he? Didn't you say you should have been so lucky? Have a man like he was?"

"I don't know how perfect he was." She sighed. "Pretty odd fellow and before the summer anyone else would have said the same."

"I guess maybe they still do."

"He left his wife and kid without much to go on, and by his own stubborn lights. Didn't he?"

"I guess so."

"And I'll tell you something else. For years I've heard you repeat the same jokes and stories in that bar, night after night."

"I know," he said. "Even the good ones are old. I haven't said anything new since I was fifteen."

"What I was going to say is that I haven't heard any of those stories in weeks. A month. You've been quiet."

"Well, it's been growing on me," he said. "Being sorry."

"OK. It's a change. Right?"

He shrugged.

"Come on," she nudged him. "Let's make a plan. Is this our home? That's Boyd's Bar across the street, isn't it? And this is the Lucy Graves."

He shrugged. "What is that," he said, "nostalgia?"

"God help me, I'm not that old and useless. I'm talking about today. Tonight. And our friends here."

"No new restaurant and pub in Burnsville."

She shook her head. "I have to stay." She pulled him toward her and he put his forehead on her chest.

"We'll stay," he said into her shirt. "Shit."

She put her hand over the top of his head. "Then let's go into that bar of yours across the street, and prop open that big old door, and open up a couple of cold beers, and turn on the radio. There's a cool breeze."

He lifted his head and looked into her eyes. "I don't deserve you."

"Deserve has nothing to do with what we get," she said, and pulled him up. When they stood, May glanced out the window and grabbed Boyd's upper arm.

"Now what in the hell," he said.

It was a truck from a Burnsville towing company hauling the Walkers' old blue Silverado through town.

"I have a feeling I better get Leigh."

Leigh swung her duffel bag into the back of Boyd's truck and climbed in the cab. May started the engine and pulled out of the dormitory parking lot. It was a picture-perfect day in mid-October and everyone was out. She crossed her arms, eyes red, and turned away from her mother. They'd been twenty minutes on the phone at dawn that morning, a call that was accusatory on May's end, defensive on Leigh's, and which had ended with an arranged meeting time on campus and without a goodbye.

They waited at a red light and Leigh watched a pack of students dressed in green and gold gear for a football game crossing the street before them, headed toward the shuttle that would take them to the stadium. All her life she was outside a window watching the rest of the world, for a few weeks it had seemed otherwise, and now she was back to where she'd always been. Outside trying to get in, and now dragged backward, back to Lions again. All of that again.

"I just want to make sure I have this timeline straight," May said, both hands on the wheel as she accelerated on the city street widening into highway. Her gaze was straight ahead, her brow furrowed. The truck was smooth and quiet compared with Gordon's. "He left two weeks ago?"

"It was like two or three weeks."

"What day?"

"I don't know." She studied the line of cheap motels and derelict mom and pop gas stations. "Middle of the month."

"Of September."

"September, yes."

"A month ago Leigh?"

"Look, mom. He's the one who left. He didn't even say goodbye, or tell me he was going. As usual. The Walker MO. Don't pretend to be surprised."

"Were you arguing?"

The cars thinned out and the motels gave way to isolated farmsteads and corn stubble. A cheerful man in a denim cap was selling cherry cider and pumpkins and waved at them.

"I'm not interrogating you, Leigh. What are you going to tell Georgie and Dock? Or Chuck?"

"Chuck?"

"We didn't wait to call him. Do you understand Gordon's been missing almost a month?"

"He was gone almost that long a couple times this summer. Chuck didn't want to talk to me then."

"He was in his truck this summer."

"And you're sure it was his truck they found."

"Leigh."

"Because John took good care of that truck. It wouldn't have just died. And Gordon wouldn't have just left it."

"It was his truck, it did break down, and Gordon did leave it."

"You're saying he just left the truck on the side of the road and disappeared into the wide open prairie."

"It looks like he must have unloaded everything first. Georgianna must have been asleep. She doesn't even seem to know he came and left again. It's a wonder none of us saw him. It must have been the middle of the night."

Leigh thought she knew which night. "The chair," she said, and could see the whole living room turned into dorm room restored to living room. She never wanted to see it again. "Well, I don't know where he is. I don't see why I need to come home."

"You didn't tell anyone."

"It wasn't my job."

"Don't you care about him?"

"He left. Again. His choice. How was I supposed to know his truck broke down?"

"OK," May said, nodding, "I'll give you that."

"He is not my responsibility."

May's eyes filled with tears. She wiped them from the corner of her eye with one middle finger, then again on the other side. Leigh turned away and looked out the window.

The sky clouded over behind them and by the time they crossed the county line the clouds had caught up overhead. It was late afternoon on a Saturday and the street downtown was empty, a few scraggly native corn decorations hung on a front door. A lopsided pumpkin on the stoop of the diner, a plastic scarecrow in front of the bar. The diner was empty except for Georgianna, who they could see from the street was refilling the glass sugar canisters at a table by the window.

"What am I supposed to tell her?" May asked her daughter. Something about seeing her old friend there, bent over in the lamplight, quickened her pulse. "That Gordon's been missing a month and no one cared enough to tell her? That now her son is gone, too, and no one knows where? That you never even called?"

"Mom."

"What were you doing all this time?"

"I was in school."

"Where you were entitled to a little fun, to a normal experience."

"Exactly."

"You act like everything happening in the world is happening in the story of your life. Leigh Ransom's precious life."

Leigh looked at her mother, uncomprehending. "If it's not my life, whose is it?"

May turned the engine off and climbed out of the truck. Boyd came out of the bar and waved at her. They met briefly in the street and May went into the diner. Leigh sat in the passenger seat with her hands in her lap. Her mother's words hung in the air beside her, but she would not look at them.

Inside Leigh carried two cups of coffee to the table where Georgianna sat. "Can I join you?"

"Leigh," Georgianna stood and spilled a good half cup of sugar down her dress and onto the floor. "It's so nice to have you back." Leigh hugged her, and held her breath in her nose. It smelled like the woman hadn't showered in weeks.

"Hi, Georgie," Leigh said.

She smiled and sat down. "Place isn't the same."

"Pretty quiet." Leigh sat.

"Your mother's still getting customers from the highway."

"I heard they're going to widen it."

"That's what they say."

"Are you going to stay here?"

"Me?" Georgianna looked out the window, then turned back to Leigh and stroked the back of her hand. "Sweetheart, there's nowhere to go."

"There's a whole world out there, Georgie. You're only in your fifties."

"Leigh thinks the world owes her something," May said. Leigh was about to fire something back when Georgianna laughed softly.

"Yes, well. She'll get over that," Georgianna said.

May went behind the counter and washed her hands. She took four heads of cabbage from the walk-in and started chopping.

"Georgie," Leigh said. Georgianna set the sugar funnel on the table. "I don't think Gordon liked school much."

Georgianna waved a hand. "I didn't think he would."

Behind them, the chopping stopped.

"Did you know he left? A few weeks ago? Left school?"

More chopping.

"Of course he did."

"Do you know where he is, though? They found his truck."

May stopped chopping.

"Oh, he's around," Georgianna said.

"Around?"

She nodded, "Course he is."

Leigh had the same sense she had on the morning of John's death. Then again on her birthday. For Georgianna, talking about her son was talking about her husband. And talking about either one of them was like talking about the quality of the air.

"Georgie," Leigh said, and caught her mother's eye. Georgianna looked up again, and waited, her gaze fixed on Leigh's. "I was just wondering if you might like a piece of pie?"

"If there's a lemon cream I'd love that." She lowered her voice to a whisper. "I made it myself, and I know it's good." She winked.

May whispered at Leigh behind the counter as she took down the lemon cream pie and cut into it. "How could you turn your back on him? Gordon was grieving." The floor behind the counter was shining. May must have been scrubbing the place raw. The stainless steel, the floors, the stove, the grill.

"I know that."

"Like hell you did. You and Boyd and Dock making up some dead man on the mesa. So full of bullshit you can't smell it on your own nose."

"I didn't believe any of that," Leigh muttered. She bit the ragged cuticle on her forefinger with her teeth.

"You what?"

"I said I didn't really believe any of that. Come on." She shut her eyes. She could see the narrow house on the mesa lit up inside her eyelids like a film negative.

"Keep your voice down. I have never seen such impatience. He lost his father, Leigh."

"You don't know how hard he made it. He didn't want me anymore."

"Didn't want you anymore? What would that have to do with anything?" She raised both eyebrows. "Besides, you were his best friend. You should have seen him the day he saw you making out with that man from Denver. He had his head on the steering wheel out there for twenty minutes. Twenty minutes, Leigh."

Leigh's face flushed and her stomach turned. John's binoculars. "You don't know how hard it was," she said dumbly. Gordon saw the man lead her into the factory. Did he see the man walk out two minutes later, alone?

"And then there was your proposal to Dex Meredith. On the day of John's service, no less."

"I never proposed to Dex Meredith."

"Yes, you did. You were drunk."

Leigh turned her back on May and looked out at the street. She put her hand on the counter and closed her eyes again. "You don't know anything about it. You refuse to see."

May circled in front of Leigh and took her daughter's chin with her thumb and forefinger. "Look at me." May's face was lined with wrinkles and spotted in new places—on her temple, on her cheek. Her eyes were a bloodshot, watery blue. The wraith of a long lost beauty looked out. "Your options aren't as unlimited as you think they are."

Leigh twisted her face away. "Don't ever touch me again."

The bells rang on the swinging glass door and Boyd stepped inside.

"Bring that slice of pie to Georgie," May said. "You're going to have to have a more frank talk with her."

"I'm all done here," Georgianna said. She stood up from the table where she'd been funneling sugar and looked across the diner at the three of them. "You know what John used to say about that mesa story? Boggs?" She smiled and crossed the room, stood beside them at the counter. They stared at her, not realizing she'd heard them. Leigh's face was red with embarrassment.

"He knew the story?" May asked.

"Knew it! John said his grandfather made it up himself, just so he could get out of the shop for a few days at a time, keep everyone away and take a break."

"The heck you say, Georgie. Walkers lived to work," Boyd said. "That was John Walker or I never knew the guy."

"But Lord could he be lazy!" Georgie said. "He could put his feet up and read three novels in a row with nothing but a can of beans, a can of sardines, and a can of peaches to interrupt him. And Gordon's the same way." She shook her head. "I don't know how many paperbacks we have in that house. Hundreds, all of them silly. Full of cowboys and gold and stagecoach robberies."

"Westerns," May said.

"Westerns," Georgianna repeated.

"Georgie what are you telling us?" Boyd bumped Georgianna's shoulder playfully with his own and grinned. "There was never any Boggs?"

Georgianna gave them all a funny look. "What," she said, "you don't mean really? A real flesh and blood ghost up there? All these hundred and fifty years?" She shook her head and looked out at the street. "Now wouldn't that be scary?"

The Quonset hut was lit up and the windows in the shop hung in the dark.

Dock opened the door. Annie stepped out from behind him.

"Have you seen him?" Leigh asked before they could say hello. They both looked at her blankly. "Gordon."

"Is he back?" Dock asked.

"Like two or three weeks ago he came back. A month maybe. I don't know. They found his truck."

"Who found his truck?"

"He hasn't been here at all?"

Emery was behind them, rocking on the workbench and listening to radio ministry. He had a blanket wrapped around his shoulders and Leigh realized the radio wasn't John's radio.

"Are you living here?" she looked from Annie to Dock and back again.

"We had a house fire," Dock said, raising his hand. "It's temporary, it's temporary. This place is Gordon's. We know that. Georgie knows we're here. Place is right and tight and it's getting cold."

"Did Gordon see you here?"

Dock put his hands up. "I haven't seen him."

Annie pulled Leigh inside. "This is temporary," she said. She put her arm around Leigh. "No shortage of empty houses around here for us to choose from. Tea? Hot cocoa? We have a hotplate."

Emery stumbled off the workbench and came to the doorway, his thumbs hooked together and elbows hyperextended. The blanket spilled around his ankles.

"I should check the factory," Leigh said. "Before it gets dark. I'm sure he's camped out there being, you know, being Gordon."

"I don't know," Dock said. "Was he OK last time you saw him?"

"He was," she shrugged. "You know. Himself. Like the summer."

"Let me come with you. It's already dark."

"It's OK."

"Leigh. You've got me worried."

Driving into town beside Dock, Leigh saw the beautiful old blue truck impounded behind chain-link with two dozen other cars and trucks in various states of rusted out disrepair. It was terrible, seeing it in a pile of junk like that, among all those discarded and unwanted vehicles. That was John and Gordon's truck. Gordon loved that truck. And he couldn't have driven north without it. Was he in a bar ditch somewhere? Hurt? Her hand went to the beauty mark behind her ear that he used to touch as he started tracing a line down her neck.

"That's his truck, alright," Dock said. He took a phone out of his shirt pocket. "Why don't we call Chuck before we do anything or go anywhere?" He pulled over. "You talked to him yet?"

Leigh shook her head. He dialed and handed her the phone. She greeted Chuck and nodded and looked from the window to Dock and back again.

"Well, have you talked to Georgie?" she asked. "And what does she say?"

"Was there anything in the truck?" Dock whispered to Leigh to ask Chuck.

"Was there anything in the truck?" She shook her head. She looked at Dock. "It was pulled over northbound on the county road between Alton's and Jorgensen's."

"No note?" Dock asked.

"No note, nothing?" Leigh said into the phone. She shook her head. She waited. "Mr. Garcia you can't auction that truck."

"Has anyone filed a missing persons report?" Dock asked.

"No," Leigh said. "Don't do that. Not yet. He'll be in the factory. Let me check. I'll call you back."

"I'm so sorry, Leigh," Dock said when she handed him the phone.

"I'm not surprised he's gone, but I don't understand about the truck."

"Georgie says he's fine."

"I know. But Chuck doesn't trust her judgment."

"We'll keep looking. We'll check your factory in the daylight, OK? If he's there, he's not going out in this."

Outside, sleet came down slantwise in gleaming needles. Back at the Walkers' shop she slipped away and crossed the yard. The sound of wind chimes Georgianna left hanging. The wind whistling through the tree in her own yard. She walked across the empty dirt road. She could see the light in the weld shop behind her and imagined that it was John Walker in there, with his wry smile, and that soon he'd be closing up and heading back to the house where he and Georgianna and Gordon would be having dinner.

She gazed over the silent field and toward the colossal ruin of the factory, where she saw, in an upper window, a flare of brightness. The light bounced into the shabby lace of tea-colored hogweed, and disappeared. She held her breath, searching the dark amorphous field, then tore the whole way across it, under the chain-link in the old place, and over the glitter of glass from Alan Ranger's beer bottles and through the door. It was pitch dark. She paused, breathing hard, looking for the stairs in the shadows, and ran to them. Up the narrow, ladder-like steps to the second story, but no, the light had been from higher still. The tower? Had he finished the steps up to the tower? She ran up one more level to the broken stairs and looked up into the darkness. Still broken. And no light. She spun around 360 degrees, twice, three times.

She went to the far east window and called his name. Down the ladder and all around the second story, calling his name, swearing at him. No light. No sound but the weather outside the broken windows.

Dock found her in a heap on the floor.

"I saw him."

"Where?"

"He won't answer." She lifted her head and called him again. Dock held still and listened.

"Come on, Leigh. It's late."

"He's here somewhere."

"There's no one here. It's empty. It's late."

"But I saw him."

"Where?"

"Up in a window. From the yard."

"You could not have possibly seen that far."

"I saw a light flash."

"Lightning."

She shook her head.

"Listen. We'll come back in the morning, in the daylight, and look through every single room. If he's here, or was here, there's no way he won't have left some sign. Mud or something, right? We'll come back in the morning. That's just a couple hours."

"Promise?"

"Of course I do."

Dock took her under his arm and walked her to his truck. He turned on the heat and handed her a dry jacket to put over her shoulders.

"Dock," she said quietly. "Do you remember telling me and Gordon about Echo Station?"

He glanced at her. "Sure. That old game."

"I did it. That same night. I snuck out of the house and I went out there and did it."

"Did you?"

"And I'm afraid, Dock."

"Leigh," he said softly. "That's a children's game."

At dawn a cold bracing wind sang over the brittle fields. The sky was the color of brushed aluminum. Dock and Leigh searched the factory and its grounds in the cold, but there were no tracks other than their own, and there was no one inside, nor any sign that anybody else had been. He was just here, she thought. He was just. Here.

"Tell me again," Dock said, pouring hot water into her teacup, "what you saw?" May was at the diner but Boyd stood behind them in the kitchen doorway, arms crossed. He locked eyes with Dock and shook his head.

"Two flashes of a flashlight," Leigh said. "Like a signal. It came out of a window and across the field."

He handed her a small glass of juice and two aspirin. "We have to call Chuck."

"OK."

"We don't think that was Gordon you saw," Boyd said from the doorway.

Leigh turned around. "What do you think it was?"

"We think you're upset," he said, nodding at his own statement.

"I am upset."

"Wherever he is," Dock said, "seems like he wants a little space right now."

"When did you see him last, Leigh?" Boyd looked at her hard. "What was the last thing you talked about?"

"I don't remember," she said. Boyd shook his head. Heat rose in her face. "What? Why are you shaking your head at me?"

"Alright," Dock said. "Let's get Annie and Emery and go have some real breakfast. Chuck can meet us at the diner."

"I don't want to go to the diner."

"Leigh," Boyd said, "this is like work. It's something we have to do. OK?"

Was she supposed to have followed him up north to see what it was all about? Then move in with him in his dorm? And now what? Chase him? Hunt him down across the plains? Move in with Georgianna in case he should show up with his dead father, for tea? Move back in with May or into the empty factory, waiting for someone who didn't want any of the things of this world? Who didn't seem even to belong to it?

She stayed in Lions another week, as long as she could without having to drop classes or withdraw entirely. For those seven days she moved back into the house with her mother and now with Boyd, and walked each morning to the diner, always looking around her, conscious of being watched, ready in every moment to hear the sound of her name, to sense his presence behind her and to turn and be folded again into his arms. How he would smell. How warm he would be. How his hands would feel like her own hands.

The days were cool, the shadows long. From her room she could see straight across the field through the thinning yellow leaves to the factory. She walked through it by day and by night. Tents and canopies of cobwebs whitened every corner and along the broken ceilings. She picked through the piles of treasure the two of them had accumulated in their childhood and stashed here and there. She turned over a broken cottonwood drum.

"I'm going to fix this," she said. The sound of her voice was small and flat in the huge open space. She set the broken drum down on the concrete floor. She trailed her fingers in the dust, along the bricks. It'd always seemed the place was crawling with life—moths, bats, mice, possums, swallows in their little clay and daub houses in the rafters. Now they were all quiet.

She called his name. She cursed him. She sat beneath their third-story lookout and drew her knees into her chest. He was a blur in her vision, a softening and brightening of the shadows until they resolved themselves into the fawn and powder blue of his old flannel shirt. He was there in her dreams on the far side of a long narrow room.

And yet for that week in Lions, it was she who felt like a ghost. May and Boyd, the Sterlings, Chuck, when he came around, even Georgie—they were cheerful and calm about their daily routines: a little hog feeding, a little welding, a little chicken frying, a little drinking, a little ticketing on the highway. They didn't talk to her much, or look at her much. They ate May's grilled cheese or meat loaf sandwiches and toasted each other in the bar, which had two new panes of glass on either side of a new door, painted a clean, smooth yellow. After dark the men would go outside and play horseshoes in the empty street by floodlight.

On the highway, someone put a ghost town sign back up, a bright one, blue and red and green—cheerful and ironic, this time, and meant only to attract customers. By day there was a steady stream of them, and May kept the old jukebox playing western tunes, for effect. "Yellow Rose of Texas" and "Tumbling Tumbleweeds" and "Call of the Canyon" and "Red River Valley" and Leigh plugged her ears when she heard it. None of those songs was about this place. Who did they think they were kidding?

"I don't like it," Boyd said after breakfast on her last day in town, his arms and elbows propped up on the driver's side window.

"I need to go see."

"If you're not back in six hours I'm sending Chuck after you."

"Six hours? There's no way he went that far. On foot?"

"I'm serious. I'll assume Boggs has tied you up and is going to eat you and I'll send Chuck after you."

"Come on, Boyd."

"I mean I'll at least want the truck back. That's a good truck."

"OK, OK. I hear you."

"Be careful."

"I will."

"Tell you what," he said, his voice softening as he looked down the road. "There's something those Walker men could see that no one else around here was ever able to see."

She stared at him.

"Those were some good men."

The words wanted to open a space in her chest that she didn't want open. "That's not how you used to talk," she said, her sentence a blade.

"The more shame on me."

"You sound like my mom."

"Pity it took me so long."

She followed the same county road north that she knew Gordon had taken time and again that summer, up through the stricken farm fields, past the old trailer and gas station where John used to bring them when they were kids, for salty tacos in greasy paper envelopes. She could imagine the feel of them in her hands, warm and waxy. Then twenty miles more, picking carefully along the unpaved county road as it narrowed and dipped and grassed over and washboarded down a plane. Then past the little homestead behind a broken shelterbelt of dead cottonwood and living buckthorn, the siding weathered to a silvery, lavender colored wood. How lonely it looked, and how beautiful.

She saw the great plates of stone uplifted in the distance that she knew Gordon had seen in summer. She drove through the same towers of granite. She saw snow—new snow, now—on the cracked ridge of the mountains to the west. She came to the North Star motel, but it was wrecked, a ruin, rotted away. On the beds through the window the blankets were water stained, the mattresses turned, everything seeded with mouse shit and torn into rags and loose fibers by their tiny claws and teeth. She drove four hours, five, darkness closing in above her, knowing Boyd would be counting the hours. She flashed her lights. She turned the radio up. She pulled over and looked around and called his name, but the wind carried it away. There was nothing as far as the eye could see. No trees. No shrubs. No birds. No telephone poles. No cabin. There was nowhere anyone or anything could hide.

It didn't happen like this. You were young and someone or something out there was supposed to give you the space to learn and make amends, to make things right. It was a big country; it was big enough to make things right. That was its promise: everything could be made new, improved, made right.

On a frigid morning in mid-December, Boyd rose in the dark and left May sleeping beside him. He made coffee in the kitchen and stood before the sliding glass doors that opened to May's gardens, chicken coop, and the endless weedy fields behind. In the distance the sugar beet factory took shape as the sky behind it brightened from navy to gray. He took another sip of his coffee, then cinched the belt on his robe and stepped outside. It was cold. The air smelled like snow, the sky banked up with thick clouds. He squinted across the fields.

Back inside he took several cans of soup, beans, and vegetables from May's pantry and set them in a paper bag. He opened the refrigerator and took out a small jar of golden jam, from the gooseberry bushes on the side of the house. It was precious fare. Coffee grounds, into a plastic baggie and into the paper bag. A mug. He opened the freezer. May's chocolate bars. One of those, into the bag. He paused, thinking. Beans, sardines, and peaches. He found the first two, but no peaches. He slipped his feet into his old, rubber-soled slippers, and walked outside.

He crossed the yard to the Walkers', his bones aching in the cold, and left the bag outside behind the shop, just beside the curve of a rusted fender skirt from a 1969 Buick Electra. When he was back in the warm kitchen, he took out a skillet and six eggs, leftovers from the pot roast two nights before, and fried it all up in a beautiful mess. By the time May came into the kitchen in her own robe, he'd set the table, poured the orange juice, and made a fresh pot of coffee. He pulled out her chair, and kissed her on the cheek as she sat down, sleepy-headed and smiling. Two mornings later, the paper bag was gone.

They didn't hear from Leigh that Christmas or New Year's. May cried over it with Georgie, their fingers interlaced on Georgie's kitchen table.

"Our kids," May said.

"I know it."

The winter passed without sight of either Gordon or Leigh, and those who remained in Lions fell into a regular pattern of visiting, of eating, of maintaining the tidiness of their homes and of Jefferson Street, empty as it was.

Boyd repeated his routine with canned goods once every ten or fifteen days through February, and then in spring and summer, taking pleasure in making new selections at the grocery store in Burnsville. Bristling sardines. Block of sharp cheddar. Bag of green apples. Once the following autumn when Boyd went to check the supply, it looked like it'd been a good month since anyone had come; the last paper bag had dissolved in rain so that the canned food labels were bleached, and some of them had crumbled and slipped off. He thought that was discourteous, leaving it all out unlabeled like that. So he began leaving the canned food and anything else they had to share in the factory itself, in an old metal dairy crate, out of the weather. Though it sometimes took several weeks, even months, eventually everything they set out was taken.

Most everyone assumed Gordon had died. He would not have left his mother, he would not have left the shop. But

Georgianna claimed to see him regularly, and she spoke freely of their meetings. Whether in snow or rain or heat, all of those who remained—Dock or Annie Sterling, or May or Boyd, or two of them together—took turns bringing her mashed potatoes and meat loaf and applesauce and pie. They took turns paying her electrical and water bills, and eventually purchasing the goods that Boyd would take out Sunday evenings, passing through the only remaining hay in the county to the line where the cultivated fields met the wild weeds and litter of the factory. He circled around the back of the old building and slipped under the fence where Gordon and Leigh used to, until he got tired of that and Dock went out with a pair of wire cutters to make a passage through the chain-link.

Within a few years Georgianna herself passed away in her sleep and was laid to rest beside John Walker, and when Boyd got sick and needed to be closer to a hospital, the lights went out in Lions. Dock helped May nail boards over the windows of the Lucy Graves and the bar, and she drove Boyd to Laramie the same day, never to return, herself. That left only the Sterlings. Eventually, Dock's hair was as white as whorled milkweed floating in the dark, early mornings, as he tended his hogs. Annie's older brother in Kansas sent money, sometimes, Dock sold his hogs, and they got by. Almost no one came to the shop anymore but once or twice a year—someone from Burnsville who knew Dock was reliable, or someone from up by Horses who needed a small job done, a trailer fixed, a hog kennel repaired. Occasionally he was given a project he didn't know how to execute, but he'd talk through the work-up out loud with Gordon or with John, and figure it out. He kept the shop clean and kept all the Walkers' beautiful machines in running order, and he kept everything where it was—never moved or touched the Walkers' coffee cups from their place on the workbench. Dock was very clear that it was he who was the visitor—the guest in that workshop, and then in the house itself, when Georgianna passed and left it to the Sterlings. He refused to sell any of the equipment, though God knew they could've used the income.

By then it was Annie who had taken over from Boyd the task of the canned food, blankets, and five-gallon water drums, though the boys, as she called them, often helped her drive out the latter on their ATVs. It was the kind of job Emery liked.

She went in all weathers, in Dock's big sheepskin coat in late fall or winter, or in summer, her nightgown sighing against her blue veined legs as she crossed the summer grass, or across the iron gray furze in February and March. In slippers she climbed the metal staircase to the first landing and left there, right by the old awl, a can of cling peaches. A can of beans. Occasionally a new warm blanket, a little firewood, a note: Thinking of you here. Beautiful sunrise yesterday morning. Supposed to be a big snow. Happy Easter. We love you.

These days, everyone's gone. If you were to take an unmarked county road off of the highway and drive north an hour, if you could find the place, distinguishable by its high rusted water tower and abandoned sugar beet factory, you could stand in the middle of Jefferson Street and hear each note from each barn swallow floating through the air like a globe of silver. In the silence between, blood singing in your ears.

For ten years, then fifteen and seventeen, Leigh didn't go back. She finished college, dated, tried on different jobs, met her husband, married, had two children—did all the things everyone does. When she heard from May over the phone, May said nothing about the Walkers. In everything her mother asked—How were the kids? How was work?—Leigh heard: I'm not going to bring it up; you bring it up. But Leigh would never, and she always had to pour a glass of white wine afterward.

"What is it?" her husband would say, jostling her arm a little, sitting down close beside her. She'd never told him much about Gordon, and had told him very little about Lions, a place of impoverishment and uneducated people—a life they both agreed she'd been lucky to escape.

"Nothing," she would say. "I don't get along with my mother."

Sometimes now, grocery shopping, or filing a bill, or scrubbing the bathtub, she looks up, her breath caught high in her lungs. She's forgetting something. She's forgotten something. She races in her mind over the list of things she'd set out to do that day, racing through the list again and again in loops until she is calmed not by the reassurance that she hasn't missed anything on it, but by the list itself. They are half as good as desire, these lists, and keep her twice as busy.

She spends a good deal of her time grocery shopping. A beautiful grocery store three-quarters of a mile down the road from the house she shares with this husband, who came from a little upper-middle-class money, and her children, who are bright and precocious. A clean living room with tiled floors and yellow painted walls and windows full of light. Granite countertops in the kitchen, a big, rustic wooden table for family meals, and the children's crafts and games. A garden out back with red tomatoes, flowers, and lawn. Green lawn. Soft as the hair on a baby's head and you could lie down in it—the kind of pasture everyone at home had dreamt of, had counted on, had every year hoped would emerge from the ground in Lions. And now here it was, green grass, all over her yard.

On occasion, the housecleaning gets away from her, and she finds over the surfaces of all of her furniture a dusty residue like a living membrane, and she hesitates to sweep it away, though in the end she always sweeps it away, her eyes fixed out the window on the street at some passing car or neighbor with a stroller.

In dreams a stiff wind, like a whisper, comes in through a crack under the door, and she wakes troubled and sets her hand on her husband's thick arm and asks no one in particular: am I awake? Terrified that the wind is real, and will keep coming, will break between all the boards and strip the house away, tumble down the smooth creamy walls and come up beneath the kitchen and front hall floor, their ochre tiles suddenly loosed like rotted teeth, rending open the walls so that her children, now old enough not to need or want her, will walk out into the huge empty field she hoped they'd never see, the wind coming and coming until what is at the heart of her home stands exposed for her to face. And the horror of it will be that it is not—as her mother had once told her—personal. There will be nothing in the wind that cares whether she has chosen the wrong life.

Because the truth is, her husband could be the most considerate lover, the steadiest caretaker, and he wouldn't be as real to her as the shadows of leaves printed by cold moonlight on her white belly and thighs, which seem as they tremble to arrange themselves in cipher spelled out across her flesh.

A message from some place or time far away.

And how unfair it was—hadn't Gordon been the one to leave her? She had done nothing wrong. She had very carefully and by much hard work created a life in which she possessed everything she liked, and kept out everything to which she had an aversion. Was there something wrong with that? She had only wanted good company in a pleasant environment. How had that been wrong? She had surrounded herself with people who made her feel good, excised those who didn't, and left everyone else in relative peace. She had been practical and decent and good—had she not?—and had made a family that was likewise practical and decent and good.

"If you follow your heart," John Walker had once told her from his reading chair, "everything lines up perfectly. Like crystals in a dish."

In remembering it, something misgives her, something knocks softly at her sternum telling her she's gotten something terribly wrong. That somehow she's missed some very small but very important thing. She goes out into the yard or playroom to look at the faces of her children—one girl, one boy—beautiful towheaded extensions of herself, fresh-faced proof of her goodness. It's a consolation she knows is running out; they don't even look up at her anymore when she enters the room.

So must every woman like her keep a secret place. An empty space perhaps unbeknownst even to her, and that grows in proportion with everything she's ignored until it hollows her out completely. She tries to fill the space with messages and signs that she sometimes catches herself collecting, as if her real life were going to take place somewhere else, some other time—later—once she's assembled all these messages and signs into a clear map, a clear set of directions. This couldn't be her life. Not yet.

Eventually, walking home from the movies with her family on a busy street lined with buildings and stores as bright as toys, she pulls her hand away from her tall, sturdy husband, and drops her arms. She ignores the child pulling at the back of her sleeve.

"Mom?" one of her children says.

"Sweetheart?" Her husband turns around and looks back at her where she is frozen on the sidewalk, a look of wonder, or terror, on her face. In her hand she's holding loosely the twine handles of a printed paper bag. Inside the bag, a yellow ceramic serving plate carefully wrapped in tissue paper. She drops the bag and both hears and feels the plate crack. What is she paying for these things with but the days of her life? The space between her shoulders burns and the backs of her eyes burn. She feels dizzy, the inside of her head emblazoned with bright white light.

She sees that her young daughter is more beautiful than she, that even as a child, it is the daughter, not the mother, who turns all the heads. She sees that her choice of husband is as good a choice as any reasonably priced purchase she's made in her life, and that all her choices have amounted to a respectable pile of props in a comfortable game of make-believe.

Before her, her husband and daughter and son are staring, their eyes wide, their hair shining beneath the lights strung among the trees along the street.

First, she'll leave them for half a day.

Then a long weekend.

Eventually, she knows, she must leave them for good.

She'll drive east through the unoccupied town, the street overrun with weeds, all the glass punched out of any unboarded windows. She'll take shallow breaths, and she'll slow to barely moving as her old house and the Walkers' come into view. She'll stop before the shop, holding a hand to her mouth. She'll walk hurriedly over the hard uneven ground and peer inside to see nothing. No machines. No coffee mugs. The interior swept as clean as the wind gusting outside its sealed-up windows.

She'll drive north, alone, up higher and higher, as she searches for a tall narrow hut. She'll look for the white circle of a man's face flashing like a light among the trees. She'll look for a blue feather of chimney smoke. She'll drive five hours, six, ten, searching desperately from behind the wheel, but she's tried all this before. She'll find nothing up there. A road sign for an antique junk store that didn't seem to exist. An old wooden spool.

It will be when she's dead-tired, long after she's given up, turned back around, and is on the county road some five miles outside of Lions when she sees it for the hundredth time: a set of silvery, dusty tracks disguised among the stones and gray weeds that run four hundred yards into a field of brush and sage and end at the old homestead.

She'll turn down the tracks before she knows why she's doing it, her heart knocking hard, already running, tripping and sprawling out on the dirt and fine gravel and prickly pear. She'll tear open her palms on the rough ground, split her lip.

That broken little house.

The windbreak of dead trees.

A single chimney pipe.

Unremarkable.

Not a place you'd even notice if you passed by.

Can hardly even see it from the road.

Not unless you're really looking.

Still, there it is, and there it's always been.

The door will be locked, but there'll be a small window, five feet from the ground. She'll just see inside. Plates of blue light shifting in through cracks in the siding, gaps that years of rain and snow and wind opened in the mortar, now here and there stuffed with rags. A faded G.I. Joe sleeping bag on the dirt floor. An old Coleman lantern, caked with dust. A pile of paperback cowboy books. A single shot glass, opaque with dirt. Dust motes slowly sinking in the light. Behind her, the trees watching from their distant posts.

When the wind and the birds quiet, she'll press her forehead against the locked door and listen for the sound of breath, of footsteps, of a hand behind the doorknob. Someone's in there. Someone has to be in there. Over and over she'll say it, then: I'm back. I'm so sorry. I've come back. Please, God. Let me in.

Acknowledgments

Tremendous thanks to Kate Johnson and Corinna Barsan; to Georges and Valerie Borchardt; to the whole team at Grove Atlantic; thanks to Georgianna Pulver, Emerson Perez, and Marybeth Sharpe, and thanks to the many who read and reread these pages and gave me incisive and generous feedback, especially Gregory Blake Smith, Kyla Carter, Katie Cassis, John Thorp, Bryan Hurt, Jeffrey Nadzam, and Jeremy Chignell. Thanks to all of my teachers in Los Angeles. As a fiction writer I've taken liberties with history and benefited from the influence of other sources. I am particularly indebted to Willa Cather (whose work inspired the story of the homeless man drowning himself in a water tower), to Jonathan Raban's *Bad Land*, to David Lavender's *Bent's Fort*, to Perry Eberhart's *Ghosts of the Colorado Plains*, and to Eric Twitty & SWCA Environmental Consultants' *Silver Wedge: The Sugar Beet Industry in Fort Collins*